P9-AQU-298

KILLER
CHRONICLES

Somer Canon

Copyright © 2018

All Rights Reserved.

No part of this book may be reproduced, distributed or transmitted in any form or by any means without the author's written consent, except for the purposes of review

Cover Design © 2018 by Lynne Hansen Design
https://lynnehansen.zenfolio.com/

ISBN-13: 978-1-947522-15-2

ISBN-10: 1-947522-15-9

This book is a work of fiction. Names, characters, places and incidents are either a product of the author's fertile imagination or are used fictitiously. Any resemblance to actual events, places or persons, living or dead, is entirely coincidental.

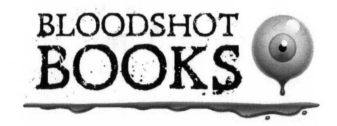

READ UNTIL YOU BLEED!

"Sexy and violent and funny...deliciously quirky." — Brian Keene

KILLER
CHRONICLES

SOMER CANON

PROLOGUE

There was a dusty, dirt path right off of the road and, desperately needing a piss, he pulled his truck onto the path. About a hundred yards in, he was surprised to see a clearing with a refreshingly clean looking pond. Usually in the heat of the summer, ponds would get covered in a thick layer of green scum and there would be mosquitos swarming all around, but this pond was a deep, cool brown. The top of the water reflected the blue sky above and cattails grew along the edges. It was beautiful.

Matt got out of the truck with a groan, his hips and back creaking from the movement. He stretched and breathed in the hot, humid air. It smelled fresh.

Fresh and young, he thought to himself.

It had been a rough few weeks since his little secret had been found out. He was awaiting trial, out on bail, for the videos and pictures on his hard drive, some of which he made himself. He'd lost his job, his wife had filed for divorce, and he was forbidden from being anywhere near his kids. He spent his days now hiding away and driving to smaller nearby towns where people might not recognize him. He'd been spit on, shoved, and hit with a shopping cart since his face had been gracing every television screen since his arrest.

He sauntered over to the edge of the pond and looked into the thick mess of cattails, hoping there were no snakes or snapping turtles. When the way was clear, he unzipped and started urinating into the water. He sighed and listened to the heavy tinkling sound for a moment. His mood lightened and he smiled. He started humming and swaying his hips, enjoying the varying sound of his stream crashing into the pond. His good mood started spreading through him, and as his bladder emptied, he could feel a warmth starting in his crotch. He smiled and stroked himself, thinking of one of his favorite videos that he'd taken of one of his daughter's friends showering in his bathroom. Memories of her soft, smooth little body just beginning to plump up with puberty made him grow rock hard in his hand.

He stood there by that pond masturbating and thinking about that girl who they now referred to as a "victim." When he finished and semen had leapt onto the cattails, he laughed heartily. He started singing as he zipped up and put himself to rights.

"Thank heaven. Thank heaven for little girls, for little girls get bigger every day!"

He saluted the cattails and got into his truck, realizing that he was hungry. He got back onto the two-lane road and drove until he happened upon a roadside shack that served ice cream and hot dogs. There was a small parking lot and picnic tables situated around the little square building. He parked and got three hot dogs and a chocolate milkshake. He sat at a picnic table where he could watch people placing orders. Not long into his second hot dog, a group of teenage girls, talking a million miles an hour and laughing about everything, bombarded the window. He sneered at them because they were loud creatures far too old for his liking. There was one, however, who caught his eye. She was hanging back from the group, a little sister perhaps. She was wearing a virginal, white sun dress and she had long, brown hair. He sat trying not to stare at her, choosing instead to place his hot dog in front of his face, right in front of where his eyes would meet her, and pretended to regard the hot dog instead of the girl. He reached up under his cap and scratched his scalp, a strange tingling sensation causing him discomfort.

I wish she was Japanese, he thought to himself. *Those little girls are always the smoothest.*

Her head turned ever so slightly and where before her hair looked brown and wavy, it now looked paper straight and black, with a pleasing sheen to it. He lowered his hot dog and took a bite, staring at the girl now.

I bet she's shy, he thought, looking at how her eyes stayed on the concrete. Her hands were folded in front of her and she swayed gently, waiting to put in her order.

She looked up at him and his heart stopped. Her eyes met his for a moment and then she looked down shyly, pushing a piece of hair behind her ear. He groaned and leaned forward, resting his elbows on the picnic table, his hot dog forgotten.

Definitely Asian, he thought. *Pouty mouth, round face, beautiful eyes. An ethnic sweet-spot.*

She darted a quick, shy glance at him again before lowering her gaze. When she left the window, she had a Styrofoam cup in her hand and she sipped delicately at the straw, looking down. It appeared now that she wasn't actually a part of the loud group of teenagers and had come for a cool refreshment all on her own. He looked around. There were some houses along the two-lane road, but there was no sidewalk. She must live close by.

She sat at one of the other picnic tables and turned her back to him. Matt tried to sit and eat his hot dog, but he was completely distracted by her. He got up and threw away the wax paper that had served as wrappers for his hot dogs and, after looking around and seeing that there were no other customers, walked over to her table and sat down across from her. She didn't look up, but he saw a pink blush kiss the apples of her cheeks.

"I have a chocolate milkshake here," he said, angling his own Styrofoam cup to her. "Do you want a sip? It's pretty good."

She shook her head slightly and continued to look down.

Goddamn, I love that innocent shyness, he thought to himself. He patted the top of his head again, the tingle persisting.

"What's that you have in your cup?" he asked her.

She looked up at him, her eyes looking frightened. He loved the feeling of interacting with a shy, young girl. He smiled warmly at her and waited for her to reply.

"Slush Puppy," she answered, her voice breathy and high.

"Oh yeah? I like those. I have a little girl about your age and her favorite flavor is grape. What flavor is yours?" He said.

He knew bringing up his daughter would put her more at ease. It made him look like less of a predator and more like a kind father who doesn't like to see a child sitting alone. A small smile curved her lips.

"Lemon lime," she answered.

"Oh, I like that taste, but I always think the color is a little too close to *snot* to drink too much," he said animatedly. It worked because she giggled lightly behind a small hand. He lost himself for a moment thinking how nice it would be to suck on one of her little fingers.

"What is your favorite flavor?" she asked him, the slightest hint of an accent apparent now that she spoke more than two words. He was close to panting.

"Cherry," he answered simply, a broad shark's grin splitting his face.

"I like cherry," she said.

I bet you do, he thought to himself. He pictured himself making her a Shirley Temple at his home bar, as he had his daughter's friend. She loved extra grenadine in hers and it always stained her lips a bright red.

"So, you live around here?" he asked, trying to look casual by taking a sip of his milkshake. "One of the houses along the road, maybe?"

She shook her head lightly.

"It's not a very safe walk along this road, is it?" he asked. "So many people drive like maniacs. I bet your parents worry about you walking that alone."

She didn't respond but kept her eyes downcast.

"I'd be happy to give you a ride home," he said. When her eyes flashed up and met his, he saw Stranger Danger fear lighting in the back of them. He smiled broadly.

"I'd hate to think of my little girl walking a road like that all by herself. I'd be really thankful to some good soul who would drive her home safely to me," he said.

"It *is* a little far," she said.

"Well come on then!" he said excitedly. "I'm happy to give you a lift!"

"Okay. Thank you very much," she said, smiling at him.

They stood, and he came around the table and stood before her. He looked down into her young face, his mind racing on where they could go and be alone.

THE POND! His mind screamed at him in anticipation. Yes, that would be the perfect place to get her out of that white dress. He was going to jail anyway. Might as well make a memory to keep him warm in there.

"My truck's over here," he said, taking her by her thin, little arm and leading her. He chanced a look over his shoulder. Whoever manned the window of the ice cream shack felt no need to be around unless there were customers right at the window. All was clear.

He helped her step up into the truck, looking at her colt-like legs as they settled before her when she was seated. He smiled up at her and closed the passenger side door. He climbed into the driver's side and put his key into the ignition, turning on the air conditioning.

"Oh geez," he said, slapping his forehead. "My manners went to the store without me, I'm sorry. My name is Matt. What's your name?"

She looked over at him and he frowned when he saw that she wore a sardonic sideways grin.

"Hello, Matt," she said in a smooth, husky voice. "My name is Grenadine."

CHAPTER ONE

I was startled out of my reading fog by the sound of Anais' forehead slamming onto her desk. I turned around in my swiveling office chair and looked at my roommate and co-worker, as she sat with her face smooshed onto her desk.

"God-fucking-damn-it," Anais said.

"What?" I asked, concern pulling my spine straight.

"That piece that the Eagle did on us is up on their web page right now," Anais said, her voice sounding funny because she hadn't bothered to remove her face from the cheap IKEA desktop before speaking to me.

I sat up straight, smiling. The piece by the local paper was a welcome bit of free publicity and the first interview from a serious paper about our work. It made me feel legitimate.

"And?" I asked expectantly.

Instead of an answer, Anais let loose a long, forlorn groan, keeping her head down.

"Shit. What?" I asked.

"That asshole made us look like psycho-loving groupies," Anais said, lifting her head. Her face was red and there was an even darker red circle in the middle of her forehead.

"What?" I asked, spinning in my chair back to my laptop. I brought up the webpage for the local newspaper and typed in my username and password for subscription access. I sat back stunned when I saw the headline of the article. **TWO LOCAL WOMEN CASH IN ON LOVE OF MURDERERS**

"Son of a bitch!" I spat.

"Read the whole thing," Anais said, burying her head in her hands and wincing noticeably, rubbing the spot in the middle of her forehead.

TWO LOCAL WOMEN CASH IN ON LOVE OF MURDERERS

Reading, PA can boast entrepreneurs in several specialties. We have local breweries, distilleries, artists, small shops and now internet journalists!

Kutztown University graduates Anais Del Valle and Christina Cunningham run the website *Killer Chronicles* (http://www.KillerChronicles.com). The site, which brags of readership all over the globe, focuses on the profiling and biographies of the nation's various murderers. The two use their journalism degrees to research, interview, and compile information in order to create what their site refers to as "files" on the murderers that they feature. So far, they have 31 files on their site.

"We have no plans to stop," said Del Valle, a Reading native. "As long as there are murderers to write about, we'll have a job."

However, not everybody sees their work as laudable. In an age where certain topics get a great amount of media attention so as to be sensationalized, *Killer Chronicles* seems to be a site that is profiting on that sensationalism. Critics of the site claim that Del Valle and Cunningham give murderers a mythical celebrity treatment on their site with little to no consideration for the victims or their families. There is worry that readers will view the murderers profiled on the site as heroes worthy of mimicry.

"Serial killers have always been sensationalized, this is nothing new. History's most gruesome moments have always gotten more attention than the good moments. While we profile more than just the serial killers, our page hit numbers speak on how interesting people of all walks of life find them to be," Del Valle said.

It is of note that *Killer Chronicles* focuses on more than your average media-saturated mass murderer or serial killer. There are files of murderers who have only one human victim. Del Valle is well aware that *Killer Chronicles* could be, at first glance, seen as a rip-off of *Murderpedia* (http://www.murderpedia.org).

"*Murderpedia* is a really great, extensive site but it's all very technical and cold, almost like public records on the murderers and their trials. We try to make our files more detailed. Each file contains several photos, interviews with witnesses and law enforcement and sometimes with the murderers themselves. Every file is almost a mini-screenplay of the murders." Del Valle explained.

Questions about ethics aside, *Killer Chronicles* is turning out to be quite the lucrative endeavor for the two women. After being online for a little over a year, the site is already selling ad space to large corporations such as McDonald's and Old Navy, a feat not even this newspaper's site can boast.

"We're thrilled with how fast we've grown. We're still a young site and since we live together and work from home, our costs are relatively low considering we travel a lot for interviews and tours of the murder scenes. Maybe next year Christina and I will make enough to get our own places," Del Valle quipped.

"Ana!" I said, turning to my roommate and coworker. "Why did you give quotes like that? You sound like a smug asshole!"

"Chris, I sat and talked with the guy for like an hour," Anais said, still rubbing her forehead. "I raved about what a great interviewer and photographer you are. I even fucking addressed the criticisms about us being inconsiderate towards the victims and their families, I really did! He cherry picked my quotes to make me sound like a jerk!"

I turned back to my computer screen and scanned over the article again. The journalist did seem to be out to shed an unbecoming light on us and our site, and the local paper, owned by an old and established family, sometimes had a tendency towards unscrupulous reporting. I closed out the tab and turned back to Anais who was now staring at the wall, her cinnamon complexion gone ruddy by the increased blood pressure thanks to anger. I'm not new to Anais and her red anger face.

"At least he didn't put our pictures with the piece," I said.

Anais snorted and looked at me.

"Oh, shut up," Anais said, throwing a balled-up tissue at me. "Don't try to cheer me up. My entire month is ruined."

"Drama queen," I teased. "Don't let it get you down. It's a local paper and it was written by some smug assface who's out to make a name for himself by trampling a couple of women trying to be their own bosses. I bet he made sexual advances to you and when you said no, he got all offended and set out to make you look bad for hurting his frail little ego." Anais laughed roughly, the apples of her cheeks scrunching her eyes in an adorable way.

"He was some middle-aged white guy with bad hair and a chewed up old pencil for taking notes. He, like so many of the old, white guys around here, looked at me like I'm some cheap *puta* and he made sure our coffee cups stayed far away from each other. I just thought he was a priss." Anais sighed. "Maybe you should give the interviews from now on, *mami*."

"Oh no you don't," I said, putting a hand up. "This website is *your* brain child, lady! You're the face of this site. We don't need embarrassment heaped on us by me sitting and stuttering and verbally crapping my way through a formal interview. I can give them, but I can't take them."

"Yeah. I guess," Anais said.

"Just admit I'm right and get over it already," I said, turning back to my computer. "We've got work to do, readers to satisfy!"

"Yeah yeah," Anais said, turning back to her own computer. "You white people are all the devil."

I smiled and began my search for the next file. Anais and I always have three files that we work on at once. We were just putting the finishing touches on a local murderess, Jessica Cortez, who murdered her boyfriend and his dog with a pair of stiletto shoes and a paint roller. It was a crime of passion. A very, very messy one (which is why it was worthy of *Killer Chronicles*). The file on Charles Parmer, the man from Nebraska who raped and murdered his neighbor's fourteen year-old son, was on hold until all of the interviews could be cemented, so a third story was needed so that new material could be posted consistently.

I have my go-to sites to check. There are sites like City-Data that have helped me in the past. Sometimes just typing "murder" or "bizarre murder" into the search bar is enough to yield interesting results. It took nearly an hour of wading through what we like to term as "typical" before I came across something that made me whistle. I turned in my seat and saw that Anais had her earbuds in, so I opened our favorite chat program and messaged Anais the link to the article. I sat back and waited.

"Jesus Hopscotching Christ," Anais said after a couple of minutes.

"I know, right?" I said excitedly. "I mean, we've covered some crazy shit, but this one is new."

"The guy was skinned. It says here that his skin was displayed in a profane manner. What the hell does that even mean? I wonder if it was a meth head or something. Down in Florida, people on crazy drugs do insane stuff," Anais said, still scrutinizing her screen, reading the article again.

"Do we not want to cover it if it's a meth-head?" I asked.

"You know, I'm not sure. I mean, the psychology of a drug-addled mind might be interesting to cover for once, but I also hesitate when it comes to someone who just flipped out while high. I mean, I'm getting crap from some newsie about our site because we're insensitive towards victims, right? I sort of feel like we'd be victimizing the drug-head. I mean, what if they came out of it and had absolutely no memory of it and they're just completely scarred that they skinned some dude? Then we come in and take their picture and shove a voice recorder under their nose and make them talk to us. I don't know," Anais said.

"Okaaay," I said. "But what if the person is insane and they think that the dude they skinned was a demon or something?"

Anais was clicking around on her computer, but she spared a moment to glare at me. Nobody likes having their logic challenged and Anais is no different. I was annoyed with that so-called journalist for causing Anais to doubt herself and our methods. If she kept it up, the process for choosing cases was going to take forever.

"Okay, the guy that was skinned?" Anais announced. "He was a child molester. He was out on bail awaiting his trial. His name was Matthew Hart. He tried to coerce one of his eight- year-old daughter's friends into touching his dick and she told her mom about it. They arrested him and got a search warrant and found out that he'd been filming kids in his bathroom. He was a fucking creep."

"So maybe this was retaliation? Or maybe some Bible-beater cleansing the earth of that scum?" I asked, rolling my chair to be next to Anais and look at her computer screen. The victim's driver's license picture was displayed. He was in his mid-30s, ruddy, but neat looking. I sneered at the picture and looked at Anais.

"It's definitely worth tagging for further investigation," Anais said. "Just keep an eye on this one. So far they don't have any real leads." Anais said.

"Right, boss lady," I said, zooming back to my desk.

I spent the rest of my working hours either on the phone or exchanging emails with interviewees in the Charles Parmer case. My policeman was starting to get squirrely and looked to be backing out and Parmer's attorney still wasn't getting back to me. All in all, it wasn't a very fruitful day. I was, however, glad that I didn't have to moderate the website like Anais. We outsourced a coder who posted ads and did the updates and such, but Anais took care of the user experience side of the site. She blocked IP addresses of spammers and bots as well as trolls and people who tried to post explicit or inappropriate content. Anais was very subjective in what constituted "inappropriate." Anything from expressing too much admiration for any particular murderer to making threats to Anais or me got people blocked from the site. Considering our growing popularity on a global scale at the time, this was enough to keep Anais strung out and stressed most days.

"I'm calling it a day and getting showered," Anais said, standing up from her chair and stretching.

"What are your plans for the evening?" I asked, stretching my legs out from a seated position.

"I got a date!" Anais said, smiling.

"Oh yeah? Where'd you find this one?" Anais has a talent for finding dates in the strangest places. The office supply store, the drive-thru window of Burger King, her optometrist's office, they are all fertile ground.

"Online, actually," Anais said, grinning shyly.

"Whoa, you had to resort to that? I thought only huge losers like me had to do online dating." I said, my eyes wide in good-natured mockery.

Anais shrugged and left the office. I put my computer into sleep mode and went to my bedroom. I plopped onto my bed and pulled out my cell phone. There were no messages from anybody I might have found interesting after work hours, so I put it on my nightstand and grabbed a book to read. I had become addicted to Urban Fantasy series books and I felt happy knowing that my night was made.

CHAPTER TWO

"**L**ooks like the child-molester-skinner struck again," I said to Anais a few days later.

Anais spun in her seat and rolled her chair to be next to me. She read the article on my screen, her lips mouthing the words as she read them.

"Wait, wait, how long was this guy missing?" Anais asked.

I elbowed Anais out of the way and did a bit of searching before finding the answer.

"Less than twenty-four hours," I said, my mouth hanging open.

"This guy was found in a local motel dismembered and turned into soap?" Anais asked, her nose scrunching up as she read the article again. "This reporter has a mole in the police force. It's someone speaking under wraps I bet."

"I bet you're right," I said. "And in a small town like this? Geez, this is crazy!"

"Alright, you've got to go over there," Anais said. "If this kind of information is getting into the paper of a little town like that, think what they're withholding. Can you imagine? Maybe we could make this one an open file and fill it in as more stuff becomes clear."

"I'm not a cop or even a legitimate member of the press, Ana," I said.

"No, but you're good with getting people to talk," Anais said, looking me in the face. "This one is too bizarre to not cover, Chris. Can you imagine the page hits we would get from people coming to the page waiting for updates? Hell, we could even name this guy! How about the Micksburg Monster?"

"The Hillbilly Hacker?" I offered.

"We'll work on it," Anais said gruffly. "It needs to sing because this might be something that could get us real attention with the *legitimate* press."

"Always about money with you," I teased.

"This one is too interesting not to cover," Anais said.

"I think I agree with you," I said.

"Then go. Your hometown is close to this place, isn't it?" Anais asked.

"Mmm, about an hour or so away," I answered.

"Do you need plane tickets, or can you drive it?" Anais asked.

"It will be about a six-hour drive. I can do that," I answered. "I'll look for a hotel right now."

Two hours later, I was carrying my big duffle bag and a smaller bag filled with toiletries to the door of our apartment, Anais trailing behind me carrying my laptop case and backpack.

"Call me when you get there, *mami*, and be careful okay?" Anais said, walking me out to my car.

"Yes, mother," I said.

"And make sure to use the business credit card for all of your expenses, I'll pay it off when it comes due," Anais said.

"I've done this before, you know!" I said.

"I know, I know but I always get nervous sending you out like this, alone and around dangerous people." Anais said. I noticed she was frowning. I frowned back in an inquisitive way.

"This one hasn't been caught yet, Chris. You're not interviewing someone chained to a chair or behind a Plexiglas barrier. This will be great for the site, but I really need you to stay frosty and alert. Don't trust anybody because I can't have anything happen to my best girl, okay?" Anais said.

"Okay, sure," I said.

"I mean it," Anais said.

"I hear you! God, calm down. I'm good at this, remember?" I said. Anais just nodded and helped me load my gear into the trunk of my modest Toyota. We hugged, as we always do when I go off on a business trip.

"I'll call you," I said, breaking the embrace and getting in the car.

"You better, *mami*," Anais answered.

* * *

The first three hours of the drive were on the turnpike. Driving on the turnpike is always surprisingly relaxing. I put on my favorite high-energy playlist and bumped around to the music, wondering why there were so many charming looking farms right off of the busy road. When I got to Maryland, I drove through the tiny town of Bedford, all two-lane roads that weaved up and around the soft, rolling mountains that I still know as home. It was on that small country road that the red Maryland road turned into pulverized West Virginia road. I got back onto the interstate and began the up and down four-lane navigation of the Appalachians. Summer was in full bloom and everything was lush and green. The GPS on my phone helped me to my destination.

My hotel was a half hour away from the crime scenes because the small town didn't have a hotel and I did not want to stay in some skeevy pay-by-the-hour motel. I like the clean consistency of a good old Holiday Inn. Well, "clean" as far as my naked, but scrutinizing, eye can see.

I called Anais from the hotel parking lot as soon as I parked. Anais was relieved and told me to keep in touch via text because she had another date that night. I shook my head, smiling. I checked in and took my big bags to my small room, smiling at the cold hominess of it. I used the bathroom and got on my phone to find a good sit-down place to have a steak. I ate better than usual on these business trips thanks to the business line of credit. Anais never said anything, and besides I thought that I deserved a steak or two if I had to do all of the traveling and leg work. I lucked out with a place that was in a strip mall within walking distance from my hotel.

I went to the restaurant, a chain place with naked concrete floors and tacky neon lights everywhere and sat at the bar. I ordered a beer and asked to see the menu, frowning that there were no ribeyes. Why call yourself a steak house if you're only serving the crappy meat that they scrape off of the floor of the slaughterhouse? Ribeyes, not sirloins, should be mandatory menu staples in all places that want to call themselves "steak houses."

I ordered a porterhouse and eyed one of the cuter waiters.

"You here on business?" the bartender asked me. She was a pretty young girl with a bad dye job and overly tweezed eyebrows.

"Yup. I'm from West-by-God, but not these parts," I answered.

"Oh yeah, where are ya from?" the bartender asked.

"Parkersburg," I answered.

"Oh, that's not far! My grandma lives in West Union, that's kind of in between here and Parkersburg," the bartender said.

I smiled at her gabbiness. This is something I know, that friendly small talk that always comes almost too close to nibbiness for foreigners. Foreigners being anybody not from "these parts." "These parts" being the not-quite urban, not-quite rural, and not at all suburban atmosphere that is the majority of the northern parts of the state just below the northern panhandle. If you didn't grow up there, you'll never get it. Don't feel bad though, you're not missing out on much. Elderly neighbor ladies who run out into their yard to stare down any car that dares drive past their house, heavy and cruel gossip at church gatherings, and having people feel comfortable asking questions of you that most polite society views as rude is not exactly a community trait that I'd call admirable. But that's just me talking. Lots of people love that kind of quaint life and choose to call it home for the entirety of their lives.

"Doddridge County, right?" I asked, taking a swig of my cold beer.

"Yup." The bartender bobbed her head, smiling.

"Maybe you can help me, then," I said, leaning my elbows on the bar and taking a more serious pose. "Where is Micksburg? I'm here researching some funny stuff that's been happening out there."

"The murders, you mean?" the bartender asked.

"That would be them, yeah," I answered.

"That's some messed up stuff goin' on out there," the girl said. I nodded seriously.

"I hear it's devil worshippers," the bartender whispered conspiratorially. I raised my eyebrows and smiled at the girl. I'd seen the devil or worship of the devil blamed on one of my other files. People are quick to blame something other than human wrath and madness on some of the horrors they themselves created.

"Well, we had us a devil worshipper thing about a year ago. A guy killed his girlfriend then himself in some sort of Satanic ritual," the bartender continued. I vaguely remembered my mother telling me about that.

"Well, I guess you never know," I said politely. The bartender nodded at me seriously.

"You just get on 51 and it's a little past West Union, right past the Doddridge/Ritchie county line," the bartender said.

"Thank you," I said.

Of course, I would use the GPS to get where I wanted to go, but I liked chewing the fat with the cute girl and wanted to see if the murders had made big local news.

Of course they had. You don't get two guys totally torn apart and put back together in fucked up ways even in big cities. Not all that often, at least.

The bartender ceased the pleasantries and let me eat my porterhouse and baked potato in peace (it would have been better if they hadn't overcooked it all). I had already had time to plan my to-do list for the trip. I had a lot to get done, and the most important things had to come first.

Number one on the list: I needed to go and stock up on Nummy Nellie snack cakes. It's something that I giddily blame on my mom, my impotence on the job unless I have a Nummy Nellie to eat. When I was young, my ongoing anxiety problems started to surface after the death of my father, so doing homework and learning new things was a big challenge for me. My mom would give me Nummy Nellie snacks "to make the experience a little sweeter, tweeter," as she said. It stuck. All through college, my mom would send me care packages containing laundry detergent, new pants, and Nummy Nellies. I love them all and would go through phases where I would favor one over the other (Stripey Cakes being the one I return to the most). In Reading, TastyKakes are the big pastry of choice, but I can't seem to fall in love with them the same way that I love my Nummy Nellie cakes. Dolly Madison also doesn't measure up. Neither does Hostess. Sure, some things are okay, but when I need that relaxation in order to get the full scale of my mind working, it *has* to be Nummy Nellie.

There was a Sheetz right next to my hotel, so instead of trying to find a grocery store I opted for the obvious convenience, ignoring the crooked glance of the cashier as I carried a giant armload of Nummy Nellies to the counter. I went back to my room and signed in to the hotel's Wi-Fi and did a few minutes of research, getting the name of the reporter that had covered the two murders and her email address. I then emailed the reporter, introducing myself and asking if we could meet the next day for lunch (I find people are more likely to agree to a meeting if I offer to pay for food). Then I texted Anais, just a quick check-in to make sure she was safe too, and when Anais told me all was well, I shut everything down and went to sleep.

The next morning, I forced myself to avoid the internet until I ventured out for coffee and a bagel. Again, the Sheetz next door proved to be very helpful since my particular hotel didn't have much to offer for breakfast and I loathe the complimentary coffee that comes in hotel rooms. The Sheetz was one of the big, shiny, new ones that had the huge selection of flavored coffees and fraps as well as hot breakfast sandwiches. I left with an enormous coffee drink topped with a nearly illegal amount of whipped cream and a breakfast wrap with eggs, gooey cheese, and sausage. I practically pranced back to my hotel room.

I opened my laptop when I was settled at the hotel desk with my treats and checked my email. The reporter had gotten back to me and explained that she was familiar with *Killer Chronicles* and would be happy to meet for lunch at the local Applebee's. I rolled my eyes at the suggestion but was happy that I secured a meeting. Number two on my to-do list was checked.

CHAPTER THREE

The lady seated in the waiting section of the Applebee's looked to be about my age. She was strikingly beautiful. She was tall and round, her hair was curly and very wide, her complexion was clear and olive-colored, and her eyes were brown and large. I put on my professional smile and strode up to the woman.

"Excuse me, are you Stephanie D'Agostino?" I asked the woman.

"Yes, I am," the woman said, standing and shaking my hand. "You're Christina Cunningham?"

"I am," I said. "Very nice to meet you and thank you for agreeing to meet with me."

"Oh, it's not a problem," Stephanie said. "I like eating lunch and you offered to buy." I laughed politely and then followed the hostess to our booth.

"I am assuming that this is about what's been going on in Micksburg," Stephanie said, browsing her menu.

"Good guess," I said.

"Well, you've made a name for yourself," Stephanie said, putting her menu aside and looking me in the face. I mirrored the action, knowing that it would keep Stephanie engaged.

"And I knew that those two weird-assed murders would have less...eh...mainstream people sniffing around," Stephanie said.

I smiled. I'd been called a weirdo before.

"My interest was piqued on the first incident, but my partner and I decided to wait and see what happened. Then, when I read about the second incident, I got in my car that day and drove down. This is certainly something beyond bizarre." I said. She sniffed and looked off to the side as if to hide an offended look on her face.

I was starting to lose my composure when the unbearably perky waiter took our drink and food orders (my thinned patience took offence with him for taking for-freaking-ever getting to our table and we were pretty much the only people there). I had to watch myself and my mannerisms. That's a fun thing about anxiety; you get really good at clenching and unclenching every single muscle in your face.

"You're driving distance away then? Where do you hail from, Ms. Cunningham?" Stephanie said in a cool professional way. I bristled. Although a bit of online digging would easily reveal that I live in Reading, I'm still uncomfortable revealing where I live. I make a living off of the predators of this great country of ours. Certain questions scare me.

"I actually grew up just in Parkersburg. I'm sort of a local girl," I said.

"Oh? Well then there's more than just morbidity bringing you here?" Stephanie asked.

"Professional calling," I politely corrected.

"If you say so," Stephanie said.

I cleared my throat, my mind working to try to get Stephanie back on track and out of her unnecessarily rude rut. Quaint curiosity is one thing, but this bitch was being downright hostile. Luckily, our drinks came and Stephanie sucked on her straw, staring me down the whole time.

"Your articles are more detailed than what I would expect from your usual small-town rag," I said. "You have more details than the official police statements would give. I know, because I've looked over a few hundred of them at this point."

"You've only been doing this for a year, Ms. Cunningham," Stephanie said. Her tone stayed polite and cool.

"But it's *all* I do," I said, holding a finger up. My patience was at the breaking point. "While someone like you might see two murders a year, I've covered over 30. In detail. I've done over 150 interviews and I've worked with a lot of law enforcement. Ms. D'Agostino, I am NOT just some smear mag writer."

Stephanie blinked at me for a moment and then nodded her head as if she had just received the answer to an important question.

"Alright, then," Stephanie said. "You can call me Stephanie, by the way. Look, sorry I got rude with you there, but I just wanted to see if you were going to get all weird murderer fan-girl on me. I've been to your site and while I don't completely agree that you aid in the hero worship of some of these sickos, I don't exactly think it's not about that either. But it *is* journalism. Your research and interviews are very good and thorough." Stephanie sat back and waved a hand magnanimously at me. "You can ask your questions now."

I had to resist the urge to scoff and leave. Instead, I smiled politely.

"Thank you," I said.

"I've been doing this for about ten years and I had to work hard to get my sources and name secured," Stephanie said. "I'm happy to help a fellow snoop."

My smile was a little sincerer this time. I understood the pain in the ass of getting people to talk to you and starting from nothing. She was still a bit of a bitch, but I had to at least respect where that bitchiness was coming from. I took out my cell phone and opened my note-taking app.

"Okay, I know you have a source in the police force who's speaking under terms of anonymity. Any chance I can get a name?" I asked.

Stephanie inhaled deeply and took another long sip of her drink.

"He's a personal friend, not just a business contact. I think I'd say no if he were only a mole." She squinted at me and then winked and smiled. "Let me text him, hold on," she said.

Our food came while Stephanie tapped away at the flat screen of her phone. I stayed politely quiet and even waited until Stephanie started eating before starting myself. Manners matter.

Stephanie finally set her phone to the side and smiled at me as she popped a French fry into her mouth. I raised my eyebrows and stared at Stephanie expectantly.

"His name is Terry Knight," Stephanie said. "We were friends in high school. I'm a local girl too. I've vouched for you, so please don't make me regret that." I was adding this to my note taking app and Stephanie even gave me Terry's phone number.

"He prefers to be texted," Stephanie said. "Just introduce yourself and he'll be cooperative. He likes talking."

"This is fantastic, Stephanie," I said, smiling and putting my cell phone back into my bag. "Thank you so much, this makes my life so much easier."

"Stay in touch. Hopefully this sick bastard is finished, but if there is something else, let's be in communication, okay?" Stephanie said.

"Sure thing," I said.

I went back to my hotel and sent Anais an update text. Then, I texted Terry Knight, and I introduced myself politely at the beginning of the first text. He replied immediately.

"Stephanie told me about you. What do you need from me?" he texted. I appreciated his getting to the point.

"I'd like to be able to see the crime scenes so that I can photograph them. I understand that they've since been cleared. I'd also like to see the reports. I'll try on my own to talk to the detective leading this case, but your help is very much appreciated," I texted back.

"I'm a nine to fiver," his next text began. "I like to have dinner right after work."

I knew he was angling to get me to offer to go to dinner. Stephanie must have told him that I was a credit card flinging bribe artist.

"There's a steak house up here by my hotel. I'm not really familiar with the area, but I'd love to treat you to a meal in exchange for some info," I texted back.

"I know the place. I'll be there at about five after," he texted back.

I turned off my phone and got back onto my laptop. I had some work to do on other files and I needed to contact an officer or detective to give me an official statement. I worked for a few hours, and then I showered and changed my clothes into something more fetching. Although I'm not every person's cup of tea, I've found that fixing myself up and wearing clothes that look professionally sexy makes people more willing to gab with me. And yes, that includes women. It's amazing how many buttoned-up women I've flirted with and gotten nice and gabby. If I can get them to gab, I can get them to answer a few more questions. I'm not happy about it, but it's part of the job of getting results. Yeah, it sets the feminist plight back about 50 years, but I've got bills to pay and interviews to do. When looks matter less, I'll be happy to conduct interviews in yoga pants and old comfortable T-shirts.

I chose a black dress that hugged my body in a way that showed nothing but curves. It was knee-length, so it wasn't advertising **SEX KITTEN** to anybody and it still looked professional. I let my hair stay down. My stark white skin and long face can tend to look a bit severe when I wear my hair back. Unfortunately, my hair wasn't being very cooperative, and it sat flat on my head, not diffusing the severity of my features at all. I tried bending at the waist and fluffing it as well as I could and when I flipped back into the upright position, it was just right. I put on a berry-colored lipstick and made sure I smelled nice and headed out to the steak house.

The steak house had a very large room that you walked into to meet the hostess that wasn't part of the eating area. There were benches along all of the walls, but there were families and small children taking up the benches. I gave the hostess my name and stated that it would be a party of two, took my red-lighted beeper thingy, and stood with my back against the wall. Every time the door opened, I would look.

Like any person who battles anxiety, I really fucking hate waiting.

The door swung open, letting in a warm breeze, and I turned and the tall man who had just walked in smiled and waved at me. He jogged over to me and held out a large hand. I took it, noting the roughness and warmth.

Oh no, I thought as I smiled up into his clean-cut smiling face.

He was gorgeous.

Dark, straight hair fell over his clean, clear forehead and deep, brown eyes squinted and twinkled when he smiled. His mouth was the devastating part. Perfectly-shaped, naturally colored lips spread over white, impossibly perfect teeth.

"Um, are you Terry?" I asked.

Great, I've turned into a stupid question asking weenie, I thought to myself.

I am not at all suave and confident around those that I find attractive. But this time, I at least had a good excuse for my bumbling. It just so happened that I was in the middle of a rather long dry spell sexually, and this tall, dark, gorgeous man was the absolute last thing that I needed on a business trip.

"Yup!" Terry answered happily. "Real nice to meet you, Miss Cunningham!" He pumped my hand in both of his. I smiled and slowly removed my hand.

"You can call me Christina," I said.

He nodded and beamed down at me. I smiled back in an uncomfortable, tight-lipped way. He took a step back from me and leaned on the wall opposite, maybe six feet away. We stood like that in the loud waiting room until the red lights flashed on my beeper thingy, indicating that our table was ready.

We sat in two hard, wooden chairs looking across a small table at each other. Terry was still smiling, and I was trying to get used to his face so that I could think clearly enough to actually talk. I coughed into my hand to clear my throat and smiled at Terry, causing him to smile wider at me.

"I really appreciate you talking with me. Of course, all of the information you give me will be anonymous," I said, noting his unadorned blue polo shirt. "Can I ask, what is your position with the police department? I mean, you're not in uniform."

"Well that's because I'm not actually a cop," Terry said. "I'm a secretary."

"Oh." I said, smiling politely. I thought that I did a good job of hiding my shock, but I was annoyed with myself for being shocked. Of course, in this day and age, the job of secretary would be for men as well as old ladies named Doris.

Terry laughed, and I knew I must have made a face.

Smooth operator, as usual, Christina. God, I suck. My mind berated me.

"I get heck for it sometimes, but I always knew I was going to be in a job that required a lot of organizational skills. It's something that keeps me relaxed, organizing and filing. The phone calls? Not so much, but the other stuff I actually quite like," he said.

"I eat snack cakes to relax," I said, glad that my natural speech had returned to me.

"Oh yeah?" Terry said. "What kind?"

"Nummy Nellie," I answered.

"Just...all Nummy Nellie?" he asked.

"Well, yeah," I answered. "I mean, I guess if I had to pick a favorite, it would be the Stripey Cakes, but I love all of them. I love Choco Crunch and Fudge Mounds and Peanutty Bars and Fudgey Rolls. It just has to be Nummy Nellie. No other brands."

"That's...that's pretty specific," Terry said. He laughed to himself. "To each his own, though, right?"

"Right," I said, smiling.

We ordered drinks and an appetizer. Terry gushed about the onion blossom and the horseradish dipping sauce that came with it, so we ordered one of those and he ordered a whiskey sour while I got a rum and Coke.

If the interviewee orders booze, you order booze too. You don't make a person drink alone.

"So, how do you get to be in a line of work like this?" Terry asked after taking a sip of his drink.

"My roommate and I were friends in college and we stayed really close after graduation. She came to me one day with this idea of profiling murderers. She had noticed that aside from diplomats and presidents, murderers tended to get the most media attention. They get book deals, biographies, movies, and even magazine covers. She's a bit of a horror lover, and she wanted to make these 'files' on each murderer where we sort of made a story out of the murders and who committed them. I needed a better job and I've always been good with interviews, so I joined her." I'd given versions of this story to almost every person I'd interviewed. Everybody seems to be dying to know the why.

"Have you met anybody that gave you the creeps?" Terry asked. I took a sip of my drink and admired the way his Adam's apple moved when he swallowed.

"It's creepy that I *haven't* met a creepy murderer yet," I answered truthfully. "By the time I can interview them, they're already in jail and are chastened for the most part. We profile people who do really horrible things, but at the end of the day, they're still really ordinary people."

"That's unexpected," Terry said, frowning.

"I agree," I said. "I expected to be talking to complete detached crazy people, like Charles Manson or something, but they're all sort of boring aside from what they did."

We sat in silence for a bit. I made an effort not to look at Terry too much. I was extremely uncomfortable, and I was pulling a really shitty interview because of it. I cursed my dry spell and had a fleeting thought of inviting him back to my hotel room and screwing his brains out just so I could think straight around him. I chanced a glance at his left hand when he took a drink and saw that his ring finger was bare. I entertained my fantasy for a moment longer before the reality of my sexual appetite hit me. If we went back to my room, I wouldn't be able to unwrap my thighs from around him for at least a week, and Anais might have had a problem with our business account paying for a hotel room just so I could have a sex marathon.

"So, Stephanie said that you two went to school together??" I asked, needing to get out of my own head.

"Oh sure. In these small towns, once you're friends with someone, you stay friends until you die or get in a fight over a land contract or something." Terry said, smiling at me. I smiled back, feeling myself warming in the middle thanks to his good looks and the rum.

"We went to school together, yeah," Terry answered. "All levels of school. She used to chase me around the playground in grade school, pass me notes in middle school, and try to get me hooked up with her girl friends in high school. I was a pathetic kid."

"How did you two get into this information exchange situation?" I asked. Terry shrugged lazily and leaned back in his chair. I swallowed hard.

"I had the job and she needed the information. I'm not breaking any rules as long as I'm not speaking in an official capacity," Terry said.

"So it's a pretty easy going situation, then," I said, bobbing my head up and down thoughtfully. "Gosh, that's nice. I have to pull out almost every trick in the book to get people to talk to me sometimes."

"I'll talk to you," Terry said reassuringly. "Stephanie said you were alright, so you don't need to charm me or drug my drinks or anything." He smiled and winked at me and I shifted in my seat, crossing my legs and squeezing my thighs together.

Christ, I'm like a cat in heat, I thought to myself. *Calm the hell down, Chris.*

"That will be a nice change, especially considering that there's no actual murderer to profile as of yet, just the murders themselves," I said, hoping that I sounded nonplussed.

"Exactly how many details do you typically like to have?" Terry asked. "I have to admit, there are quite a few things that were kept out of the papers because there was some seriously sick stuff at those crime scenes, and I know that not as a cop or detective, but as the person who files away the reports and overhears talk."

"We like to be pretty detailed, actually," I said. "We're not going for gore porn or anything but the professional, clinical reporting on the murders doesn't make for very good reading."

"So, it's for entertainment purposes then? Your website?" Terry asked. I frowned.

"Yes and no." I said. "That's not an easy answer. I mean, we do want to hook people and we do take pictures and get as many of the horrible details as we can, but there's seriously a lot of work that goes into what we do. My partner, Anais, says that we are writing little biographies on the murderers and that it's not sensationalism. Like how people can write books about Jack the Ripper and include actual pictures of the victims and crime scenes while they were still fresh, and those books are seen as almost intellectual because a lot of research goes into them. I mean, we don't include pictures of the crime scenes until after they've been cleaned up, and although I have seen a few pictures of the dead bodies, I would never ever post them on our site." Terry smiled broadly and pointed a finger at me.

"We have something in common," he said. "We both catch heck for what we do."

"Is it obvious?" I asked, smiling down into my drink.

"Oh yeah," Terry answered. "I can tell you've had to defend your job many times."

"Yeah, well," I said. "We get some pretty awful allegations thrown at us."

Terry gave me a sympathetic half-smile. The onion blossom came, and he dug in with enthusiasm. I tried to restrain myself and eat delicately, because this was still essentially a business dinner. Terry noticed my dainty nibbles and that I would only take the tiniest dabs of the horseradish dip. He frowned and chewed at me for a minute before pointing a finger in my face.

"We have a lot to cover. We're going to be talking quite a lot. I can't be comfortable around someone who isn't comfortable themselves," he said. "I saw how your nostrils flared when this was sat on the table. Look at this thing," he said, gesturing to the battered, petaled, deep fried monstrosity that was easily the size of a large dinner plate. "There's lots here and I don't want to eat it all by myself. Please, eat it with me and stop picking at it."

I frowned at him, having a moment where I took sincere offense to what he said. I looked at him staring back at me, eyes wide and chewing happily. I picked up another petal of onion and did an obnoxiously hearty dip into the horseradish sauce and jammed the entire thing into my mouth.

"Happy now?" I said through the mouthful of food. Terry burst out laughing and gestured to the waitress to come back to their table.

"We're going to need more of the dipping sauce," he said. "There's no way this little cup is enough."

I smiled despite myself.

Charming and good looking. Damn it.

CHAPTER FOUR

I was sitting on the hood of my car waiting for Terry to meet me in the parking lot of my hotel. It was early Saturday and when we had had our dinner on Thursday over large plates of food, we planned to meet then so that Terry could drive with me to where Matthew Hart's remains were found. I argued that I could use my GPS to find the place, but Terry told me that the place was off-road and down a dirt path and that if I weren't with someone who knew what they were looking for, I'd never find it. I'd managed to convince myself that that was a good argument, but the fact of the matter was, I was hoping to spend more time with the cute guy. Like a damned teenager, I was looking for any opportunity to be with my crush, and I was even playing the helpless little lady to boot. If I thought about it, it made me mad. So I was working to not think about it.

I was entertaining the idea of going to the Sheetz for a breakfast sandwich when Terry's F-150 pulled into the parking lot. He parked near me, got out, and sauntered over to me. I sat up and smiled at him, seeing that he was carrying two coffees in a carrier and a box of doughnuts. He was too good to be true. What with the tight T-shirt stretched across his broad chest and the well-fitted blue jeans, I was never going to be able to think straight with him around.

"I can't start a day without something in my stomach," he said, extending one of the coffees in my direction. I accepted it with what I hoped was a restrained smile.

"Well thank you," I said, examining the doughnuts in the box. They were cake doughnuts in different fruity flavors with a shiny glaze making them glow in the morning sunlight. I grabbed one that I hoped was blueberry and took a bite and smiled at its sweetness. Terry was watching me, and he smiled before grabbing a strawberry doughnut and eating nearly half of it in one bite.

"I really appreciate you doing this," I said to him. "I got a hold of the state police yesterday and I couldn't get anybody to talk to me on the record or off."

Since the local police was such a small force, there were no investigators and certainly not anybody trained to investigate a couple of particularly heinous murders. I had had to go through a stressed-sounding secretary to a very annoyed sounding detective to a severely hostile sergeant.

"Yikes," Terry said, swallowing the last of his doughnut and looking at me over the lid of his coffee cup as he took a drink. "That's too bad they have to be like that. You might make them famous."

I snorted a laugh and picked another doughnut, my hand bumping into Terry's as he grabbed for the same one. Terry smiled and gestured with his hand that I could have it and I accepted it with a nod.

"I doubt I could make them famous" I said. "It's not a new thing for officials to be wary of speaking to me and since this is an ongoing investigation, I knew that my chances were a lot slimmer than usual. It's a mild annoyance, that's all. But I'm not making celebrities out of these people. It's not all ambition and political agendas, you know."

"So, you don't get cops hamming up for television cameras and hoping to run for Congress or anything?" Terry asked. I looked over at him, trying to gauge what he was getting at, but he just seemed to like gabbing while he ate.

"Not really," I answered. "They are usually tired of talking about it to be honest. A lot of them see those investigations as traumatic experiences to their departments and to their towns. They don't see it as star-makers like television would have you think. Nobody wants to look at some of the things those men and women have to scrutinize."

"I never thought of it that way," Terry said. "But I can see that now. From what I've heard about the murders that have happened here, I can say with all seriousness that I'm glad that I just file things away and answer phones."

We finished off the box of six doughnuts and got into Terry's truck with our coffees. He put on the radio and played country music. I crinkled my nose and looked out of the window, making mental notes about where we were going in case I wanted to come back on my own without Terry clouding my ability to think like an intelligent being.

Damn dry patch, I thought to myself.

We drove on a small four-lane highway for about a half hour before turning off and driving down a two-lane road that seemed to be a tunnel through thick forestation. About three miles down that road, Terry slowed way down and started looking off to the right. I watched the right and Terry turned off on what looked like nothing more than a beaten path through the brush. He drove for a bit and we ended up in a clearing that ended with a beautiful, large pond.

"Wow, this is really gorgeous," I said, pulling my DSLR camera out of my bag.

"Yeah. Nobody seemed to know that this place was here. By the time Mr. Hart's truck was found, the skin was rotting and falling apart. It looked like some small scavengers had been at it too," Terry said, getting out of the tall truck.

"Who found it?" I asked, walking around, looking for the best angle to show the serenity and beauty of the lake. Beautiful places were always a great thing to photograph because people could hardly believe that horrors had happened among such loveliness.

"We got an anonymous tip. A phone call," Terry said.

I spun around and looked at him. I ran back to my bag in the truck and pulled out my voice recorder. The blouse that I was wearing had a breast pocket, so I turned on the recorder and stuffed it in the pocket so that I could record the conversation for note taking later.

"Okay, I'm talking to my anonymous source at the scene where Matthew Hart's truck and remains were found. I'm told that the remains were not exactly fresh. They were chewed on by the local wildlife and had begun decomposing. The scene is off of a small, rural road that is nothing more than a path where the weeds are beaten down by the few car tires that have ventured out this way. At the end of the path is a small, but beautifully clean pond. I'm told that the remains were not discovered by a civilian, but that an anonymous phone call was placed to the police," I said. "Was the call to the state police or to the local station?" I asked Terry.

"The local station," he said. I was happy that he said it loud and clear so that the recorder would pick it up. I needed loud clear talking to hear over the rustling that would be recorded from the recorder being in my pocket.

"And can you tell me what you know about what was found here?" I asked, seeing the pond from that perfect angle and snapping a few pictures.

"Well, from what I understand, after the call was put in..." Terry began, but I had a thought and had to interrupt.

"Wait, wait. I'm sorry, but were you the one who answered the phone call?" I asked.

"I was not," Terry answered.

"Do you happen to know the gender of the person who phoned in the tip?" I asked, walking around Terry's big truck to get a picture of the path that led to this rural oasis.

"Yes. It was a woman who phoned in the tip." Terry answered.

"That's interesting," I said. "Please continue with the description of how things were found. Sorry."

"That's alright. You think on your feet," Terry said, winking at me. He had to stop it with the winking. It was too damned cute.

"Okay, after the call was received, a single officer in an official vehicle was sent to the scene. He apparently had a heck of a time finding the place because the description was so vague. See, we could see the path a little better today because of all the vehicles that've been in and out of here lately, but it was much harder to see for our man. When he finally did find it, at first he saw what he thought was just a really dirty Dodge pickup truck. When he got out of his cruiser, the smell tipped him off that there was a body nearby. It had been hot, and the smell was quite strong I'm told," Terry said.

"The newspaper said that there was human skin stuck to the outside of the truck?" I said. I wanted to keep my thoughts straight so that when I was taking notes from the recorder later, I could keep everything linear.

"Yes," Terry said.

"Where was the rest of him?" I asked.

"None of that was ever found," Terry answered. "All we ever got of him was the skin."

"And how were you able to get an identity on the victim?" I asked.

"Well, the truck belonged to the victim, and he had an identifying tattoo on his left arm. His face was also still intact and left on the inside of the truck. His bondsman was able to identify those parts," Terry said.

"Can you tell me about the skin and the face, please?" I asked. I was still snapping pictures as he talked. I like to have a lot to choose from.

"Well, his entire body was skinned. Even his hands and feet. It was ripped into pieces and stuck all over the outside of the truck. His face was the only part that was left on the inside. Like I said before, it was pretty gross by the time it was discovered."

"Do they know how the skin was removed? Was there any evidence on the skin of stabbings or a gunshot wound?" I asked.

"No, nothing like that," Terry answered. "The findings seemed to conclude that the skin was *ripped* from the body. There are no marks that would indicate that a cutting tool was used. The skin was ripped into the smaller pieces that were used to coat the truck. Someone very strong did this."

"What are the theories on the cause of death?" I asked. I'd stopped taking pictures and was looking out at the serene brown water of the lake.

"He was alive when his skin was ripped off of his body. Mr. Hart's cause of death is believed to be flaying," Terry said. I smiled because Terry had done a very Scooby-Doo-esque gulp before saying "flaying."

"That's awful. I know that man was no saint, but that's a horrible way to go. Was this the scene of the murder? Surely there was blood and bio matter everywhere," I said.

"This was not the scene of the flaying, no. Everything was clean save for the truck," Terry answered.

"That's curious. That brings up a million questions about Mr. Hart's truck. Was it left here and decorated later or is there perhaps more than one person involved in this?" I asked more to myself than Terry.

"I don't know that one," Terry said.

I was still looking out over the water, trying to think but I just couldn't seem to concentrate. Something about the place made me peaceful and happy. I was almost relieved when Terry's cell phone rang, and he excused himself to his truck to take the call. I grabbed my bag and plopped my butt down by the water. I pulled a pack of Stripey Cakes out and opened the cellophane. I sat eating the cake and looking out over the water. I was so happy that I couldn't resist singing.

"A pack of love, a pack of happy, share a cake and make it snappy! Nummy Nellie is love for the belly!"

I realize now that perhaps I have a problem with Nummy Nellie in that I actually went to YouTube and looked up a Nummy Nellie jingle from the 90s. I sing it in private happy moments. The absurd happiness washing over me at that moment seemed to pull that tune out of me. I sang quietly, hoping Terry wouldn't hear my ridiculousness. I reached down beside me to get the second cake from the package, but it was gone. The cellophane was still there, but the cake was gone. I wondered if perhaps, in my Nummy Nellie revelry, I had eaten the other one in a mindless stupor.

I got up and stood by the water's edge, not wanting to look too approachable and casual for Terry. I was still in "professional" mode. When his phone call had ended, he rolled down his driver's side window and stuck his head out.

"Is that all that you needed from this place?" he asked me. I nodded in the affirmative. "I'll take you to the motel where the other body was found if you want."

"I appreciate the offer, Terry, but really I don't want to take up your whole weekend." I said.

"Think nothing of it. I'd just be sitting on my rump watching baseball right now anyway. Come on," he said.

I climbed up into his truck and placed my bag on my lap chastely and smiled at Terry.

"Okay then. Let's go," I said.

CHAPTER FIVE

Terry parked in front of the Green Hills Motel. As far as local motels go, this one was just plain horrible. It was a one-level place with only about twelve units, all of them shaded by the surrounding overgrown trees. It was built into and thrived on privacy. It was a place to bring drug-addled prostitutes and shame your grandparents. My skin itched just looking at it.

"Well this place is nasty," I said to Terry. Terry laughed.

"It ain't a local treasure or anything," he said.

I climbed down from the truck and walked way out to get a wide shot of the whole structure and then got a shot of the rusted-out neon sign that probably flickered at night. Terry followed me as I walked to the main office. I took pictures of the entrance and then of a row of doors from a side angle. I walked into the office and flashed my brightest smile at the plump woman behind the desk who looked like she lived inside of a miasma of cigarette smoke. She was a Misty Rose kind of lady, just like my mom.

"Help you?" the old lady said in a scratchy voice without looking up from the paperback she was reading.

"Yes, ma'am, you can," I said in my sweetest voice. That got her to look up at me. She noticed Terry standing beside me.

"Rate's $65 an hour," she said, looking back down at her book. Terry cleared his throat in discomfort.

"Oh, no ma'am, we're not here for a room," I began. The lady dog-eared her page, slowly closed her book, and lit up another of those skinny, pink cancer sticks.

"So yer one of them weirdos who's lookin' to see where they found that guy in room eight?" I could see how greasy her hair and face were now that she was looking directly at me. I was standing a few steps back from the front desk hoping to avoid the cigarette smoke, but I could smell her even from there.

"Not exactly, ma'am," I said, trying to look completely unruffled. "My name is Christina Cunningham. I am a writer for the website *Killer Chronicles* and we have decided to cover the horrible things that have been going on down here."

I pulled out a business card and handed it to her. She glanced at it and threw it on the desktop, taking a long hard drag off of her dainty smoke and exhaling out of the side of her mouth. Her fingernails were yellow, and I could see black gunk underneath. I started to get anxious at the thought of having this woman touch me.

"Sound like a weirdo to me," the woman croaked.

I started to feel like my smile had been carved into my face. Sweat was beading on my forehead at the thought of the smell of this woman seeping into my clothes.

"I was wondering if you could answer a few questions for me and possibly let me take a few photographs of the inside of the room where the remains were found?" I said, trying to control the conversation.

"I ain't lettin' you into a room just to take pictures of it," the woman said, waving a hand at me dismissively.

"I could let you speak on the condition of anonymity," I said. "You wouldn't have to hurt your business. Or I could take your picture to put along with your interview if you'd like a bit more involvement. I really only have a few questions and just one quick picture of the inside of the room would really be enough."

"Ain't no point in speakin' anonymous-like," the woman said. "I own this place and I's usually the one here at the desk. I got a friend who comes sometimes when I need a break, but I's the one that's here. My maid found what was in that room, came and got me, and when I saw that there was human bones there, I called the police. Ain't much else to tell."

"I really do appreciate you talking to me, ma'am," I said. "Would it be alright if I recorded this so that I can keep everything straight?"

The woman waved a "don't give a shit" hand at me. My eye caught on an old dirty bandage wrapped around the tip of one of her fingers. I pushed the button on the small voice recorder and held it out in front of me in a defensive gesture.

"Could you please tell me your name, ma'am?" I said.

"My name is Katherine Hardesty," the woman croaked. She wiped a hand across her forehead and then wiped her hand down the front of her yellowed T-shirt.

"And the name of the maid who first found the remains?" I asked.

"I ain't comfortable giving you names of people who might not want to be in your website," Katherine said.

"Okay, I understand," I said. I then recounted what Katherine had already told me into the voice recorder.

"Can you give me any details about what you found in the room, Ms. Hardesty?" I asked.

"At first it just looked like somebody left some trash behind. That happens sometimes. The bed was still made, and the bathroom was still clean. Nothin' was mussed. There was just a pile of soap bars on the TV stand and something on the bed that looked a bit off. I went and got a closer look and saw that they was bones all piled up nice and neat. It weren't the first time somethin' like that was left in one of the rooms. Had a dead baby left in the toilet once," Katherine said.

I made a sour face.

"Did the room smell odd? Did you touch or smell the soap bars?" I asked.

"The room smelled like it always smells. There weren't no dead guy smell or nothin', I did pick up one of the bars of soap and give it a sniff. It looked and smelled like that homemade artisan shit you overpay for at craft fairs. I didn't think nothin' of it until we found the note," Katherine said.

I perked up. There was no mention of a note in the article in the newspaper.

"Can you tell me about the note?" I asked calmly.

"Yeah. It was left by the phone. I found it when I went to call 911. It was written on some sort of leather or funny thick paper. The handwriting was really messy, like they was writing with the hand they don't usually write with, you know? The note said something about the guy being a filthy creature and he was made into somethin', so he wasn't a waste on the universe no more. It was like a poem."

"Did the police say anything to you about it? I'm assuming they interviewed you?" I asked.

"The boys that came down here weren't too talkative. They wanted to know things like times and who checked into the room last. I wasn't much help," Katherine said.

"Why do you say that?" I asked.

"I ain't runnin' a boomin' business here or nothin', but I get enough people in here that I don't remember faces. The logbook says that that Hamrick man checked in to room eight and paid for only one hour. I made a note that he had a guest, but for the life of me, I don't remember seeing neither of them, even though I was the one that was here," Katherine said.

"And how long after Mr. Hamrick's hour was up did your maid go in to clean the room?" I asked.

"She went in a little over an hour after his hour was up," Katherine answered, lighting another Misty.

Is there anything else you'd like to add, Ms. Hardesty?" I asked. Sometimes I use the personal thoughts and conjectures of the locals to add a bit of color to our files.

Katherine stared at me thoughtfully. I noticed that there was brown grime in the folds of her neck.

"My old granny used to make soap. It took weeks and she didn't need to get her fat off a person like this loon did. I ain't got no idea how his bones was stripped clean and turned into soap in a little over two hours, but I tell you what. I make sure to get a look at every person who wants a room now."

I heard Terry shuffle behind me. I turned slightly to chance a glance at him and his studious cleanliness made my stress levels go down about twelve notches. I gave him a half-smile because he was obviously very uncomfortable. Maybe it was the dead baby bit, I don't know. All I know is that I was in a full hangover sweat from looking at that filthy woman and I wanted nothing more than to leave, but I needed to try to get her to let me photograph the room.

"Ms. Hardesty," I began. "Thank you so much for talking to me. Now, while my voice recorder is still going, will you tell me if you prefer to speak under anonymity or have your name published along with your statement?"

"Ya can use my name, I guess. Can't hurt nothin'," Katherine answered.

"Again, thank you. Would you like for me to take your photograph and have it along with your statement as well?" I asked.

"Nah," she answered simply.

"Alright, then," I said nonchalantly. I was happy not to have a photographic reminder of her grossness. "Ms. Hardesty, before I came into this office, I took some photographs of the front of your establishment. Would it be alright with you if I used them on my site?"

"Yeah, I guess," Katherine said, scratching under her chin and making a face similar to one a dog makes when you scratch its sweet spot.

"Might I ask again if I can photograph room eight? I don't need to touch anything or take more than two or three photos. It will all take less than five minutes," I said. I really wanted photos of the inside of the room. Even after the horrible things had been cleaned up, showing our readers photos of the crime scenes was something that got us those sweet, sweet page hits.

"Aw, hell," Katherine said, angling herself sideways and launching herself from the chair. She pulled a key out of a drawer and walked around the side of the desk and indicated the main door behind me. I stepped out of the door, closely followed by Terry, and Katherine came out last, shuffling and huffing her way past us. I got another, stronger whiff of her and bit the inside of my cheek to keep from making a face. Katherine led the way as we walked under an awning that covered chewing gum and cigarette butt littered concrete. She stopped in front of one of the dirty, green doors with a tarnished, bronze number eight on the front. She used a metal key to unlock the knob and swung it inward, staying outside and gesturing for me to go in.

The floor was a brown-stained, tight-pile berber carpet. The walls were painted a dingy, sky blue. The bed had two flat pillows at the head and the bedspread was an old thing with bright greens and yellow flowers that I'm pretty sure my grandma had in the seventies. It smelled stale, the way a room that sees a lot of smoking and screwing can smell. There was the odor of Lysol trying very hard to cover up that bodily fluid/post-coital cigarettes smell, but it wasn't trying hard enough. I made quick work of getting photos of the bed and television table. I walked out of there, past Katherine, as fast as I could. I stood on my own off to the side and Terry began walking towards me when Katherine put a hand out that landed on his chest.

"If ya'll need anything else, I guess ya can come back and ask," Katherine said seriously.

"Thank you," I said. "I really appreciate your help, Ms. Hardesty."

Terry nodded at Katherine and smiled down at her politely. He stepped to the side to get her hand off of him and she smiled at him. That was all I could take of the woman. It was the first good look that I got of her teeth and it was more than enough. I turned immediately and walked out to Terry's truck and waited for him by the passenger door.

I was leaning against the side of his truck holding my middle and wiping sweat from all over my face and neck. It wasn't a full-blown anxiety attack, but it was close enough that I needed to decompress. I held a hand up to Terry as he approached me, concern all over his face and walked towards the tailgate of his truck and called Anais.

"Hey," Ana said after the second ring. She knew it was me.

"Ana," I said.

"Chris," Anais said, sounding concerned. "What happened?"

"I did an interview with the woman who owns the motel where the second person's remains were found and...I sort of lost it. She was dirty, Ana. She was so dirty. She smoked and she had dirty nails and her teeth... I swear there was actual gunk on her teeth, Ana."

"Okay, okay," Anais soothed. She got calls like this from me often enough to know how to talk me down. "Talk to me about what you're finding out," she said, changing the subject.

I filled her in on the new developments and what I had gotten down so far. I had enough material to write and post the first installment of the file. Anais was very pleased, and that made me feel better. She asked me where I was heading next and I told her that I wanted to meet with the cleaning crew that had Matthew Hart's truck and with Martin Hamrick's girlfriend. "Okay, now, are you feeling better?" she asked me.

I took a deep breath in and my heart didn't try to burst out of my chest.

"Yeah," I said.

"Talk to me, *mami*," Anais said. "You doing your footsteps? Eating alright?"

My "footsteps" is something that I do to keep myself sort of even. I have one of those fancy pedometers that you wear on your wrist. It's digital and syncs up with my phone to let me know how many footsteps I get in a day and how many active minutes I've had and all of that fun stuff. It's a distraction that also helps me to keep a handle on my weight considering I have a predilection towards a diet that would make a cardiologist shoot me.

"I didn't make my footsteps the day I drove in, but I paced around my room enough yesterday that I got to ten thousand. I'm pretty sure I'll get them in today, too," I answered.

"And how are you eating?" she asked, knowing perfectly well that I was worse than usual when I traveled.

"I'm being pretty bad, actually," I admitted. "Lots of steaks and pastries."

"Gotta cut that shit out," Anais said sternly. "You're going to keep getting worked up if you're not taking care of yourself and if you come home and see that you've put on weight you're going to really get upset."

"I know," I said, sounding pouty.

"I know you know," Anais said tartly. "I need you to take care of you. Okay? If you need me, I'll drive down. I'll leave right now if you need me."

"No," I said. "I've got it. I'm going to straighten up and get back on the wagon."

I was engaged a few years prior to this point to my long-time boyfriend Isaac. He was my prom date and my first love. We lived together for a few years and had almost settled on a date for the wedding.

I think that little problems exist in every relationship, but it's the little problems that we are hell bent on ignoring that turn into the fatal sword strikes that eventually kill anything that was ever good in that relationship. Our fatal problem was our sex life.

When I lost my virginity, it felt like a levee broke and flooded everything around me. I'd never known a high like the high I got from sex. When I first got with Isaac, he considered himself a lucky guy to be with someone who couldn't seem to get enough of him. As the relationship aged and mellowed, his feelings switched. He couldn't keep up with me or keep me as satisfied as he thought he should have been able to do. I really tried not to put pressure on him about it, but every time I tried to initiate sex with him and he wasn't up for it, he became resentful. That little problem sat in the middle of our idyllic life and festered until he couldn't take it anymore and he started a relationship with some girl from his job. He couldn't keep up with me sexually, so he decided to have sex with someone else. That turned my life on its ear. I couldn't understand how my wanting him had driven him away and I became fixated on injecting my life with routines that would have predictable outcomes. I needed A plus B to always equal C. My weight was the biggest and easiest target for my fixation. Counting calories and meeting a certain footstep requirement made me able to control and maintain that number on the scale. Once I relaxed enough to allow for that extra pound or two around my period, it became my sense of safety and security. Predictability is an anxious person's favorite teddy bear.

When Anais and I had ended our call, I got into the truck with Terry. I looked over at him and smiled politely.

"Thank you so much for bringing me out here. This was a very fruitful day." I said.

"Are you okay?" Terry asked me, putting a cool hand on my shoulder.

I looked over at him and had a conversation in my head at light speed about how personal I wanted to get with this guy.

"I'm fine," I said, smiling tightly.

"Are you sure?" he asked. He frowned at me and he got a wrinkle in between his eyebrows that I caught myself staring at.

"Yeah," I said, shaking myself out of it. "I just have anxiety issues sometimes and that dirty woman started getting to me."

Terry chuckled and started the engine. We had light chitchat while he drove me back to my hotel. When he was parked, I reached for the door handle when he put that cool hand back on my shoulder.

"You'll get in touch with me if you need anything else, won't you?" he asked.

"Terry, I'm not even close to being done with you. I'm going to need to talk to a few more people, but then I'm going to want to see the police reports, or at least interview you and get a quick synopsis on them," I said.

"So, we're going to still be seeing a lot of each other?" he asked.

"We'll be in touch by phone at the very least," I said, digging through my bag for my room key.

"How long, exactly, do you think you'll be in town?" he asked.

I looked up and into his face. I'd paid for my room for six days, but I knew that I'd most likely stay a bit longer. I didn't really want to tell him that.

"Until I've got everything that there is to get," I answered coolly.

"Oh," he answered quietly.

I looked at him again and frowned.

"What?" I asked.

He sat for a moment, adjusting his body and fidgeting before saying anything.

"Well I feel like a scum for saying this," he began. I made a "get on with it" motion with my hands and he cleared his throat dramatically.

"I like the look of you," he finally said. "I think you're pretty and I think you're nice and I like watching you work. I know you live like four hundred miles away, and I'm not proposing marriage or anything, but I was just wondering if you'd like my company while you're in town."

I sat blinking at Terry for entirely too long before it was my turn to start fidgeting and coughing dramatically.

"Terry," I began. "I'm not even going to be here that long and I'm here for work, not pleasure."

"I get that," he said. "But you've got down time too, don't you?"

"Well yeah," I said.

"Well, maybe you'll think about spending some of it with me." I opened my mouth to say something, but he held his hand up and stopped me. He leaned over and opened his glove compartment and pulled out a small notepad and a pen. He wrote something down and tore the sheet off, handing it to me.

"Look," he said. "I'm going to get a table for two at this place at seven o'clock. That's enough time for you to think about it. I'll wait until eight o'clock. If you don't show up, no problem, I'll still work with you and I won't be a jerk to you. But if you do show up, I think we could have a good time together."

I sat for a moment, thinking about what he'd said and wishing that I'd had the guts to say it first.

"Okay," I said. "I'll think about it."

He smiled brightly at me and I climbed out of his truck and walked into my hotel. I was waiting for the elevator when I noticed a little girl standing by a big, plastic plant close to the lobby. She was dressed in a blue and white plaid dress with puffy sleeves and a big, poofy skirt. She was also wearing a blue bonnet that covered her ears and her blond pigtails trailed down her arms. I thought she must have been dressed for a recital or something because a person wouldn't dress like that for casual life. The girl turned her head slightly and looked at me and I gasped.

Nummy Nellie was in my hotel lobby and she had just winked at me.

CHAPTER SIX

I got composed enough to think myself stupid for actually thinking that Nummy Nellie was stalking me (I've said before, my love borders on psychosis for those snacks). The girl's resemblance was very uncanny, however, and I decided to go to her and tell her so.

"Hi," I said to the girl brightly. "You know, your little dress and bonnet makes you look just like Nummy Nellie. Is that on purpose?"

The girl, who looked to be eight or nine years old, pursed her lips and looked into my face.

"I thought for sure that this is how you'd want me to look," the girl said in a surprisingly husky voice.

"Uh, do I know you?" I asked, completely confused.

"Christina," the girl said in her very adult voice. "Why does nobody here seem to know what they're doing when they come to my pond?"

"Your pond?" I asked. "What are you talking about? Are you here alone? Where are your parents?"

The girl held up a finger and I watched as it turned from a small pink digit into a grotesque, elongated, craggy gray finger with a curved claw at the nail. She pointed the talon at me menacingly.

"I doubt you want to talk to me in front of so many innocent eyes," she said.

"I doubt I want to talk to you at all," I said backing away towards the stairs. To hell with waiting for the elevator.

"But we're going to talk, Christina," the girl/thing said. "You sang your soul to me. You even left me a gift."

"What in the hell are you talking about?" I asked, but as soon as the words flew out of my mouth, some of it became clear. That pond. The Nummy Nellie jingle I sang. The missing cake.

"What the...?" was all I could manage to get out.

"Your room, Christina," the girl/thing said to me.

I nodded dumbly and turned to lead the way to the stairs. I was on the fourth floor and I took the stairs by twos to get out of the stairwell. The girl/thing stayed right behind me the whole time. It took me two tries to get my stupid key card to unlock the door but when I did, I stepped into the room and held the heavy door open so that the girl/thing could come in as well. She glided in past me and I caught a whiff of wood smoke and chlorophyll from her. She smelled like sweet green things and a warm hearth. It was nice.

I didn't know what to do, and the girl/thing seemed preoccupied with examining my hotel room, so I sat at the desk and watched her, wondering what was coming next. She went into the dark bathroom and came back out looking less like Nummy Nellie and more like the owner of the freaky finger she'd pointed at me. She stayed short, but her skin took on a wrinkled, saggy quality. Her nose was a bit longer and pointier and the radiant, blond pigtails took on a quality of black, wet mop strings.

"The others had a lot of questions, but they were scum. You?" The girl/thing came and stood by me and stroked my hair. I tried to sit still and not lean away from its touch.

"I'll answer your questions," the thing finished.

I didn't know where to begin. Who? What? Why? Nummy Nellie?

The thing laughed like it was reading my thoughts and sat on my bed, facing me.

"Ask," it demanded, gesturing with its long finger.

"Uh," I said. "What is your name?"

The thing frowned. It wasn't in an angry way, but in a way that made it look confused. It sat for a moment, tapping its chin with its talon before looking me in the eyes. The eyes had gone green. Not green like eyes are usually colored, I'm talking you get a box of crayons and find the one labeled simply "GREEN" and that was its eye color.

"I don't remember my name," it said finally. "I was alone for so long that I'd forgotten it, and I can't remember anymore. I've been telling your type that my name is Grenadine."

"Grenadine?" I blurted.

"I saw red lips and innocence lost in that name. But the word is pretty, isn't it?" Grenadine asked.

"I guess," I said.

"Ask." Grenadine said again.

"Are you human?" I asked, leaning forward in my chair.

"Gods, no," Grenadine answered in disgust.

"Then what are you?" I asked.

"Now *that* I remember," Grenadine said. "I used to keep my pond in another part of this world, but I moved when people stopped believing. If I was going to be ignored, I was going to have peace. I always liked keeping a doorway to this world. It's so ugly here and without ugliness, I couldn't truly appreciate the beauty of my home. You humans are pathetic, weak, owned by fragile egos, and very much willing to bend to superior beings. Some people thought of me and my kind as mischievous. I guess when you steal a few babies and trick a few stupid young boys into taking on giants you get a bad reputation. The thing was, it also got us reverence, something we didn't get much of in our home plane." It stopped talking and got a wistful look on its face. "That was all so long ago. Back when I still knew my name. Back when there were more of us and the giants still lived. I don't think those of us that remain were meant to endure for as long as we have. Immortality and solitude are hard to live with when you've been worshipped and revered in centuries past. And here you are, a complicated thing and you knew to sing sweetness and to leave a gift to the fairy of the water. I haven't had that since I came here."

"Fairy?" I asked.

"I am one of the *wee people*, as we were once called," Grenadine said.

A dark thought hit me. A scary thought that I was terrified to voice out loud. I scratched at my head, annoyed at a strange tingling sensation.

"They were low forms of human, which is already a low form of life," Grenadine said. She was definitely reading my mind. She was admitting to me that she was the killer of Matthew Hart and Martin Hamrick.

"You don't call upon a superior being with no offering. The first one, the one that brought me over for the first time in centuries was a predator of children. He cared only for his own hide, so I liberated him of said hide and decorated that garish truck of his with it. The other one was a drunk who liked to beat and urinate all over his woman. When the universe belches out a filthy creature such as that, it's only fitting that they repay the people that had to endure them by cleansing their presence away," Grenadine explained.

"That's why you made soap out of him?" I asked.

"I left some for everybody, but I sent a bar special to that woman of his. The best part of that is that even after she learned what it was, she didn't turn it in to the authorities. She used it. Very circular and very beautiful," Grenadine said.

"That's messed up," I said, forgetting myself. Grenadine laughed again.

"I like you, Christina. And since you've called me and given me such a nice gift, I will pay it back to you. A favor is what I owe you and I'll have to think long and hard on something appropriate."

"Like a wish?" I asked.

"I am not a genie," Grenadine said, sounding angry. "You gave me my proper dues and because of that, I'll honor you with something. A favor from a fairy is nothing to be taken lightly. It's nothing that you'll ask for, it's something that I'll see you need and give it to you."

"Are there any more of you?" I asked.

"NO MORE QUESTIONS!" Grenadine screamed belligerently. "I am not your servant, human! I came here to favor you! Can you not see how that is a blessing! Do you not know how to act among your betters?"

"I...I'm sorry," I stammered. To say I was scared shitless at this point would be an understatement. I had no idea how I'd lost Grenadine's good graces so suddenly.

Grenadine got up from my bed and stalked to me. She got in my face, our noses nearly touching. I stared into those leafy green eyes, trying not to blink for fear of missing something coming at me.

"I could take you back with me and do what I did to them," Grenadine growled at me. "My stew pot has been full ever since. I haven't eaten so well since the Banshees favored only a few families."

I swallowed hard and continued to look into the fairy's eyes.

"Don't forget yourself with me ever again," Grenadine said, standing up straight.

When her eyes were no longer inches from mine, I felt free enough to blink and breathe. And a blink was all it took for Grenadine to disappear from my room and leave me on my own. I plopped back into my chair and stared at the empty space that she had just occupied, my brain taking a little vacation from the overload. When my thinking capacity came back to me, I jumped up from my chair and ran to the bag that I had dropped by the door, got my cell phone out, and texted Anais.

"OMG you won't believe me," I texted.

As I waited for her reply, I sat and thought. She wouldn't believe me. After the phone call with the mini-anxiety attack, she would think that I was having some sort of breakdown. I'd never hallucinated before or thought I saw fairies, but even my dense brain could tell that this was not something that I could share with my supportive friend. But how was I going to handle all of this on my own? How in the hell was I going to keep writing on this file? How was I going to handle being on the radar of something that saw me as an insect?

"?" was all that Anais texted back. It was basically her way of saying, "go ahead..."

I sat with my mind racing, and I remembered Terry and his proposal.

"The secretary for the police that I've been working with asked me on a date and pretty much proposed that we be fuck buddies while I'm in town," I texted.

"Is he a creep?" Anais replied.

"I don't think so," I said.

"Then go for it. You haven't had any in a while and this might help ease some of that pent-up tension of yours," she said.

I shook my head, trying to get my thoughts straight. Did I dare start a sexual fling then and there? Was I even going to be staying?

"Will you have the first post of this file written up and posted by dinner time?" Anais asked me.

We'd already spent a good deal of money and time on this. Anais was right in that this could drive a huge amount of traffic to our site. I already had a lot of juicy stuff and photos to put into this first installment, and Anais could take to our social media accounts and really sell it.

"Yeah," I replied.

"Great. Just let me know when it's up and call me tomorrow," she said.

I went to the hotel's gym and got on the treadmill for an hour with my voice recorder playing my interviews through ear buds. Since I was only walking, I could make notes on a notepad set on the control panel of the treadmill. I got my footsteps in and I outlined my post.

I went back to my room and wrote out the first installment of the file that at that point was being called the Micksburg Mangler. I am a huge sucker for alliteration. My only regret about it was that I couldn't pull out one of my big girl words. I think all writers like to do that sometimes, use a big impressive word. Well I do, at least. It keeps me from feeling like a kid parading about as an adult.

CHAPTER SEVEN

I felt weird going on a date in blue jeans and Converse, but I didn't bring many dressy/professional clothes with me and I didn't want to keep adding to my dry-cleaning pile. I at least had on a button-up shirt and not a T-shirt.

I showed up at seven o'clock on the nose. I thought about showing up a little late to make Terry sweat, but punctuality is really important to me. People who are late bug the ever-loving shit out of me.

I found Terry sitting at a small, bistro-style table sipping a beer. When he saw me, he honestly looked startled before he scrambled to his feet and pulled my seat out for me. I had a broad, stupid grin on my face as I sat down.

"I didn't know if you'd come or not!" he said, almost gushing. "I just now got here myself."

I waved a waiter over and ordered a vodka and diet coke. I needed some liquid courage.

"I didn't want to make you wait," I said, feeling shy. We weren't there in a work-related capacity, so I couldn't keep pulling my serious act on him.

"I appreciate that," he said before taking a drink of his beer.

I watched his Adam's apple bob as he swallowed. I also noticed his still damp hair and his clean, crisp shirt. He'd put almost as much effort into this date as me. After I'd texted Anais to tell her the post was live on the site, I took a shower and made sure I was shaved and smooth and smelling fresh.

Smelling nice is a big deal to me, something which tends to make me neurotic. I remember my mom telling me, "You can always lose weight, wear better clothes, fix a bad hair day, and cover up a big zit, but if someone gets a whiff of you smelling bad even once, they'll always remember you as being a stinky person." Now, I know that's not exactly right, but it sunk in and the thought of being remembered as a smelly person terrified me enough that I never leave the house without doing a thorough sniff test of my various parts and making sure nothing offends. People who have allergies tend to not like me so much because I do wear scents, but I am careful not to overdo it and send the local bird population into a perfume-induced coma.

I wondered how he smelled. I started imagining how warm his chest would feel pressed up against me. I wondered how tight his ass would feel and if he was a deep kisser. When my drink arrived I threw it back, my throat aching from the cold.

"Since you invited me out, I'll let you pick up the check," I said, getting up. Terry looked confused and hurt.

"Then meet me at my hotel room," I said, smiling.

"But don't you want anything to eat?" he asked, thoroughly flummoxed.

"We'll order pizza. Come on, this was your idea. I don't want to draw this out and risk awkwardness," I said, spinning on the ball of my foot and leaving the restaurant.

I drove back to my hotel at an almost criminally slow speed and then took my time getting to my room in order to lessen the amount of time that I had to wait for Terry to show up. I laughed at myself for being so impulsive, but I was counting on him getting that check paid and driving to the hotel like he was on fire and I was water.

I went into my little bathroom and brushed my teeth again, fluffed my flattened hair, and paced around the room wondering if I should answer the door naked when my phone pinged, alerting me to a text message.

"I'm in the lobby and you didn't tell me your room number!" It was from Terry.

"Shit, I'm stupid," I said to myself as I texted him my room number.

I paced around my room a couple more times when the knock came. I opened the door and grabbed Terry by the front of his shirt and pulled him inside, smiling like a lunatic. He stumbled into the room and after I had shut and locked the door, I turned on him and began kissing him. He was surprised, but like me, he was there to play.

He was warm and fuzzy, and he smelled fresh. His calloused hands never lingered in one spot of my body for long and he had obviously made a study of kissing as a teenager by the way my body was reacting to even his pecks.

I had his shirt off and his pants unzipped before he returned to the moment enough to speak to me.

"This is better than Christmas!" he said, a huge smile on his face. I laughed and dropped to my knees in front of him, tugging at his well-fitted blue jeans to get at the prize hidden beneath.

I wasn't able to spend much time showing off my oral fireworks before Terry sucked in a breath between his teeth and pulled himself away from me. He leaned down, took my hands, and pulled me to my feet. I used my hand to keep playing with him.

"That's great, bless you, but if there were other uses for this fella' before the night was over, maybe we should give him a break and play with you for a bit," he said.

I shrugged and stepped away from him and undressed myself, giving him another show. He stayed back until I was completely bare. He just stood there until I invited him over with a finger. He came at me slowly, penis pointing right at me, and he actually picked me up and carried me to the bed. That was new for me and I was giggling like a kid at a clown show.

He plopped me onto the bed indelicately and I bounced back into him and our heads bonked, making us both see white for a second. We laughed and held onto the sore spots until I started stroking him again, not wanting the moment to be gone. He moved my hand away and started kissing the nape of my neck; you know, the universal ON button for almost every human vagina on the planet. I wiggled beneath him, trying to touch him more, but he deflected me. I must have gotten him very close.

He moved down to my breasts and had fun with those, kneading them with his hands and sucking lightly at the nipples. He started kissing down my stomach and I felt his hand lightly stroke up the inside of my thigh. When he kept kissing down, I grabbed him gently by the ears and angled his face back up towards me.

Look, I just don't like it. It's messy and I think it makes things stinky. I liked that he was a giver and didn't shy away from that act, but it's just not something I can sit still for. We've established that I'm neurotic, and this is just another thing to add to the list.

He came up to me easily enough. We kissed some more, with him trying very hard to keep himself pressed up against my thigh rather than the wet spot it really wanted to find. I handed him a condom that I'd put on the bedside table and he looked at me in disappointment for a minute. I pointed at the small package sternly and he started to tear it open. I laid back and watched. There's no arguing with me when it comes to condoms and safe sex. I enjoy casual sex, but I want it done in at least a physically healthy way. I'd gotten grief about it before. Some men find women who have their own condoms to be offensive and unpalatable. I detest that. I'm just taking a bit of control and if a man doesn't want to play by those rules, then he can enjoy playing pocket pool with his blue balls on the drive home.

When Terry was sheathed and I knew that I was protected, I sat up and pushed him down onto his back.

He slid in easily and I began grinding on him. I didn't take my time once he was inside of me. That familiar urgency and ache inside of me kept me from restraining myself at all. If he weren't wearing a condom, he might not have lasted long enough to get me to the end. Luckily, he was wearing one because I don't negotiate with guys sporting boners.

I felt that quickening and leaned back and gripped his thighs as I angled myself just right for that final finish. I lifted off of him and slammed back into him a few times and as I came, I squeezed his thighs a little too hard. I could hear him yelling "OW OWOWOW" through the haze of my orgasm and I leaned forward and rode him to his own finish, which he met in a disappointingly quiet way.

I fell off of him to the side and lay next to him panting and smiling, fully relaxed for the first time in days. I leaned over and stroked his softening penis and he pulled away self-consciously and got off the bed.

He was walking to the bathroom when he stopped. It wasn't a pause or a thoughtful halt, but a total freeze on his part. He was mid-step with one foot extended, ready to meet the floor.

I felt an arm drape across my stomach and I looked over.

Grenadine was in bed with me.

"I haven't seen that done in quite some time," she cooed.

I yipped and launched myself away from her, which sent me flying off of the bed and onto the floor, landing on my shoulder in a painful thud. Grenadine rolled over onto her side and looked down at me from the bed.

"I knew I liked you, but I didn't know how much I was going to like you," she said to me.

I had nothing to say. I'd just been kicked out of my post-coital glee by something looking like a mix between a Halloween witch and Nummy Nellie.

"You used him expertly, Christina," Grenadine said to me, slithering off of the bed and coming to sit next to me. She reached a hand out and stroked the skin just under my left breast. "Very nice," she said.

I rolled away from her and grabbed Terry's shirt and covered myself with it.

"I hate modesty, Christina," Grenadine said, sounding annoyed with me. I kept my nakedness hidden and Grenadine rolled her green eyes at me and reclined back and looked at Terry's frozen form.

"I have a feeling about this one, Christina," Grenadine said. "He might be the favor I pay you. Maybe he'll be something I take home to put into my stew pot." Grenadine squinted and the skin at the tip of my scalp got tight.

"He's got secrets, but he's boring," Grenadine said, waving a dismissive hand at Terry's back. "There are better specimens to use who might actually scratch the awful itch you always feel. He'll be overwhelmed by you too."

"Good thing we agreed to make this a casual thing," I said in an angry and defensive voice.

"Casual doesn't have to mean boring," Grenadine said.

Again, I had nothing to say. I was scared right out of my head and I wanted nothing more than to run out of that room, leaving Terry behind in his stasis. I started sliding my arms into the cool arms of Terry's shirt when Grenadine charged at me and ripped the shirt off of me and from my hands. She pushed me in the middle of my chest and I fell back right on my butt and looked up at her, my eyes wide and afraid.

"I said stop," Grenadine growled.

She got down on all fours and crawled over to me, her hand landing on my ankle and sliding up my leg, venturing towards my inner thigh. I scooted away, slamming my legs shut and turning to the side to keep that part of me away from prying fingers.

"I could demand recompense for this rudeness, Christina," Grenadine said, settling her hand on my lower stomach. "We used to demand first-born children. Oh, how I miss having your young around. Fairy babies aren't pretty like human babies and they certainly don't taste as delectable. Human babies were my favorite meal in my younger days. The way you animals breed, I barely put a dent in your population by feasting on a few soft, buttery babies a year. Maybe this interaction will result in a child and I can have my favorite braised baby and carrots. I haven't had that in centuries, Christina. It really is delicious."

"I'm on the pill," I said. My heart was beating fast and my breathing was coming in shallow gasps. I was lying on the horribly patterned carpet of a hotel room with a fairy hinting that she wanted to eat my offspring with a side of carrots. It was surreal. And terrifying.

Grenadine was looking at me intensely and that tightness in my scalp returned.

"Birth control, eh? That's interesting... and disappointing." She said to me.

"We try not to breed like rabbits anymore," I said, hoping to keep her in a level mood.

"And yet some of you collect pets," Grenadine said, looking past me. "The way some of you treat each other as opposed to how you treat animals is baffling. There are people who are brutes to man and beast and there are those who treat animals better than they'd ever treat a fellow human. Why is that, Christina? Why do you put your sick and infirmed on life-lengthening drugs that do little more than prolong misery and pain, yet you euthanize sick pets to ease their pain? Where is the humanity in a decision like that? Are you afraid to let the people die for fear of your own mortality or are you just quickly disposing of sick pets so that you can skip off to get a brand new one? I don't understand."

"Pets are family," I said, trying to keep up with her subject-jumping rambling.

"Pets are lesser creatures!" Grenadine snapped, pinching the skin of my stomach painfully. "Just as you are beneath me, Christina. You are worthy of my affections, but you are still a baseless beast that does little more than crawl about this earth wallowing in your own shit and eating and destroying everything around you simply because your brain doesn't seem to grasp consequences unless it involves personal, physical pain."

She pinched me harder and I was biting the inside of my cheek to keep from crying out. Her talons were digging into my skin, and I felt when the delicate tissue finally gave way. Her gray talon sank into me. I gritted my teeth and made a pained noise, pushing my eyes closed as tightly as I could. When Grenadine released me, I opened my eyes to watch her lick the blood from her talon. Her tongue was a startlingly bright red as it darted out of her mouth quickly to get at the blood, not unlike a cat lapping up milk.

"Your taste is sweet, Christina," Grenadine said, smacking her lips. "Lucky for you, I prefer savory meals."

And she was gone again. I heard Terry continue his walk to the bathroom just behind me and I scrambled back up onto the bed and under the covers. I looked at the hole in my stomach. It was an inch-wide gash weeping blood and puss. It hurt like all holy hell.

Terry came out of the bathroom a minute later, naked and shy, and started dressing himself. I sat in bed watching him, not really seeing him. I wanted to go home and get the hell away from that place and the fairy, even though I thankfully knew that she had no interest in eating me.

Just any babies I might someday have.

And Terry.

"You still want to get a pizza? I'm fine with pizza, but we can get other stuff too. There's a wing place just down the street from here that's pretty good," Terry said to me.

He came over to me and kissed me lightly on the lips and I was horrified when I felt my loins fire up again. Maybe Grenadine was right about me being a base and lesser creature, but I knew this sexually timid man wasn't up for anything other than food, so I agreed that wings sounded fantastic. I got out of bed, not ashamed of my nakedness and went into the bathroom to get cleaned up and make sure I smelled fresh.

And bandage up the hole in my stomach.

CHAPTER EIGHT

The next day I found myself standing in front of a building on a main street reading probably one of the most non-ironically hilarious signs I'd ever seen.

STAN'S SUPER SCRUBBERS

'When a mop and bucket ain't gonna cut it!'

This was the business that handled the cleaning of Matthew Hart's truck and was also the employer of Martin Hamrick. I had spoken to the owner, a Stanley Cogar, and was told to come right in for an interview. I had high hopes for a juicy interview, as Stanley sounded like a jovial and talkative gentleman over the phone.

An electronic bell dinged when I opened the door. The place was a bare-bones front office that reminded me of the place that I went to get my car maintenance done. The floors were bare concrete and the desk sitting directly opposite the front door was a metal relic that was in marvelously good condition. A small, boney, middle-aged woman sat behind the desk shuffling papers, but she looked up and greeted me with a kind smile.

"Help you, hon?" the lady asked.

"Yes, my name is Christina Cunningham and I have an appointment to speak with Mister Cogar?" I said sweetly.

"Oh, of course," the lady said, scrambling out of her seat and coming towards me. She shook my hand vigorously and smiled up into my face.

"I'm Bertie Cogar, Stanley's missus," she said. "We're happy to answer any questions you might have."

Boom. I swear I heard angels singing. It's almost never that easy.

"I really appreciate it, Mrs. Cogar," I said, smiling my best and brightest.

"STAN!" Bertie bellowed over her shoulder.

"WHAT?" Stanley bellowed back.

"GET YOUR BEHIND OUT HERE NOW!" Bertie demanded.

I heard a loud groaning from the back and a heavy metal door opened off to the right and in walked a wall of a man. He was at least six and a half feet tall and the gnarled joints on his enormous, calloused hands spoke of a life of manual labor. His immaculately clean and combed white hair contrasted with the stained and grimy blue jumpsuit he had on over his clothes.

"Stan, this is that girl who was comin' to interview you about Marty and that truck," Bertie said to him, wrapping an arm around Stanley's waist.

"Oh, yeah I remember," Stanley said, pulling a clean red bandana from his back pocket and wiping his clean hands before shaking my hand. I liked Stanley a lot.

"Mister Cogar," I began. "Thank you so much for agreeing to see me. Now before we begin with the interview, I was wondering if I might take a few photographs of the outside of your establishment? I'd also like to give you and Mrs. Cogar an opportunity to consider having me photograph the two of you to go onto the site along with your interview. This is 100% optional."

"Sure you can take pictures (she pronounced it 'pitchers') of the outside of the place," Bertie said.

"I ain't much comfortable with havin' my picture taken, though," Stanley said, looking sheepish. "I don't mean nothin' by that, but havin' my face on the internet seems a bit more of me on there than I want."

I smiled and nodded, resisting the urge to inform Stanley that almost all of his personal information could be found on the internet. It was no use with older generations, though. To many of them, the internet was something to be feared and avoided.

"That's no problem at all," I said brightly. "If you'll just give me one minute to take pictures of the front of the building, I'll be right back."

I spun and went out front and snapped a couple of pictures of the façade of the building and came back in to see

Stanley sitting behind the metal desk and Bertie sitting on top of it, holding Stanley's hand. I smiled at the sweetness of the scene and strung my camera around my neck.

"I suppose you'll be wantin' to get pictures of that truck, too." Stanley said.

"You still have it?" I asked excitedly.

"Yep. It's out in the yard here," Stanley said, rising slowly from the Bertie-sized chair and leading the way out of the door that he had entered earlier.

Bertie and I followed behind Stanley as he slowly sauntered through what looked and smelled like an equipment room. There were huge steamers, shop vacs, buckets, and jugs of differently colored cleaning solvents stacked next to boxes of face masks and latex gloves. Bertie caught me turning my head to look at all of the stuff and put a hand on my shoulder.

"It's a nasty job, but my Stan works hard at it and makes a good livin' from it," she said.

"I don't doubt it," I said, smiling down at her.

Stanley opened another heavy door that led to a back yard. There was an old Dodge pickup truck parked there and it looked to be in the process of a massive sanding and paint stripping. There were patches of the original true blue colored paint, but most of the truck was sporting the dull gray of the metal that made up the body of the vehicle.

"Did the, uh, the organic matter eat away at the paint job?" I asked.

"Naw," Stanley said, rubbing the back of his neck pensively. "This thing sat in the hot sun for a few days with them chunks of skin just cooking on it. By the time the cops took what they wanted, and we started peeling the stuff off, we could see that there was no way we was going to be able to clean it off. It was just a baked-on mess. We're just gonna strip all of the paint off and sell it off as is. Had to completely clear out the cab too. I tell you what, that was a hell of a smell."

I started snapping photos of the truck. When I went to get some snaps of the inside I saw that Stanley and his team had indeed stripped everything out. There were no seats, no upholstery, nothing. There was nothing but bare metal everywhere. I looked over at Stanley and Bertie and smiled, putting the lens cap back on my camera. I pulled out my voice recorder and waved it at them, asking if it was okay to record the interview. When they gave their consent on the recorder, I turned it on and stuck it in my breast pocket.

"There wasn't much flesh in the cab though, was there? I mean, surely there's not a lot of flesh on facial skin?" I asked.

"A boy I once worked with one time left a half-eaten hot dog in his car for a week," Stanley said. "That one little piece of hot dog, sitting in a hot car and rotting away, created a stink so hellish that it made your eyes water. I 'bout smacked the spit outta that boy's mouth. Same with this. That little bit of meat just kept getting hot and cool, hot and cool, and it smelled up that truck so bad that when the first cop on the scene opened the door, he up and puked right next to the damned door. We had to scoop that hell up before we could even start on the truck."

The saliva in my mouth had gotten thick and I swallowed hard, trying to get my throat clear.

"Can you tell me about what the truck looked like on the outside? It seems that the skin was more or less ripped from the victim instead of cut." I looked at Bertie, embarrassed. "Oh, I'm sorry. If this is too detailed for you..."

"No, no," Bertie said, waving a dismissive hand. "Honey I hunt with this man of mine and I've seen and done my share of cleaning, gutting, skinning and killing. I work the desk here because I get all claustrophobic in those breathing masks. Unless you start talking about dog shit, you're not going to upset me."

I smiled at Bertie, feeling a sense of admiration for those two humble, no-nonsense, awesome people.

"Well I apologize for the assumption," I said. I turned my eyes to Stanley and raised my eyebrows, indicating that I was ready for his answer.

"If they say the skin was ripped off, I believe it," he began. "I mean, skinning isn't really a very messy thing. With a deer, you've already gutted the thing before you start in on skinning and you just start by cutting a starting spot at the neck and you rip and cut down. But with this poor fella, it was just a bunch of, well I'm not sure. They were little pieces about the size of a sandwich, just smooshed all over that truck. And yeah, they were ragged and there were a few really thin strips in some spots. I don't even know how you'd rip skin up like that. Even without a good knife, once you had a good opening in the skin, it wouldn't take more than time and some strong arms to take the skin off like a T-shirt. Maybe it was ripped up after it was removed." Stanley shook his head and patted Bertie on her cheek, smiling down at her.

"The face was probably the part that upset us all the most," Stanley continued. "See, I'm one of only two cleaning specialists with a permit to clean places contaminated with biohazardous waste in this area. And I've seen some stuff. But the way that man's face was ripped off of his head, God, his eyelids were still intact. His beard scruff, his eyebrows and eyelashes, even his ears, they were all perfectly intact and just spread out pretty as can be on the dashboard of that there truck. Even the part of the skin that had the tattoo. You could fool yourself into seeing those pieces as something other than what they were, but that face sitting there all half rotted and slimy staring up at me...I don't think I'll ever forget that."

I looked over into the truck again and saw that the plastic or fiberglass dash cover had been ripped out. I was never going to hear the phrase "baked on" on those stupid dishwashing commercials and not think of this truck ever again.

"Would you like to speculate on what happened to the rest of Mr. Hart's remains?" I asked.

I don't know why I asked. I knew where he'd ended up. I'd heard Grenadine's sultry phantom voice say the words "stew pot" at least a million times in the past two days in the nightmare producing part of my subconscious. I kept picturing a huge, black, cast iron cauldron sitting over a fire with gory bits of meat and organs floating in an orange broth.

"Not really," Stanley answered.

I could tell by the way his mouth was scrunching up, that he was going to speculate anyway. Unsavory material or not, this man had opinions to share.

"The way I see it, that fella was killed somewhere far from where that truck was found. There would have been one hell of a mess wherever he was killed. Now I been thinking about it and I figure whoever did it has a place all their own out somewhere quiet where they did this. I mean, with a deer, it takes time to gut and skin. If you can get it hung up on a tree, the gutting can go a little quicker, maybe 15 minutes, but it still takes an hour or two to skin the thing and we usually don't rip up the skin to smear all over a perfectly good truck. It's a messy job. I got no idea about what this maniac did to the rest of the fella. Maybe they buried it. Maybe they put him in a big freezer and saved him for later. Sick people don't seem to know no limits."

"Okay," I said quietly. "Thank you. Now can you tell me a little bit about Martin Hamrick?"

Bertie groaned. Stanley rolled his eyes and looked down, not meeting my eyes. I frowned in a "let me in on the secret" way.

"We don't mean to disrespect the dead," Stanley said.

"The man was strange," Bertie finished.

"Strange?" I prompted.

"He had a drinking problem," Stanley said. "He came in to work once or twice still pickled and I had to threaten to fire him if he did it again. I try not to be too hard on alcoholics. I've known more than my fair share. Besides, in these parts, if alcoholism is the only disease you got, you're lucky." Stanley rubbed the back of his neck again and looked down at Bertie. There seemed to be a conversation going on with the significant looks they kept shooting each other.

"He was a little awkward, I guess. He had himself a girlfriend. Nice girl. Never understood why she was with Marty," Stanley said.

"He was a filthy person," Bertie said in an outburst. "He had the means to be a clean person, but he always smelled just awful and he was mean as a snake to boot. I didn't wish the man dead, please believe that, but I'm glad I don't have to ever be in his presence again."

Stanley exhaled loudly and glared down at Bertie who returned his glare for everything she was worth. Apparently, there was a difference of opinion on what "respect for the dead" meant and Bertie didn't hold to it as strongly as her husband.

"Was he a good worker?" I asked, moving things along.

"He showed up when he was called, that's about all I can say about that," Stanley answered.

"Was he with you to get Matthew Hart's truck cleaned up?" I asked.

"Yep," Stanley answered. "He was pretty upset over that and had to go sit down by that pretty little pond there by where the thing was found. He eventually came back, smiling like a jack-o'-lantern. Said that that pond made him feel real happy and he got to cleaning like he never cleaned before. I was impressed."

An icy sensation started creeping up my spine.

"Was it the next day that he missed work?" I asked.

"Yep," Stanley answered. "Never saw him again after that. I got the truck towed over here, nobody could stand sitting in it with that smell, and he helped me lock the place up and that was the last I saw of him."

"I do hope that this hasn't had a negative effect on your company," I said, meaning it.

"Naw, we'll be alright. Lots of people need a job and this isn't one that requires a college degree," Stanley said, smiling at me.

I reached into my pocket and turned off the voice recorder. I walked to the Cogar's and shook both of their hands, thanking them sincerely for their time and information.

"It's no problem, honey," Bertie said. "You're nicer than that girl from the paper. She was smarmy and borderline rude when she interviewed my Stan." Bertie wrapped a protective arm around her enormous husband's waist and smiled up at him fondly.

I frowned lightly. Yes, Stephanie D'Agostino had a bit of an attitude, but she and I were not in competition with each other either. She was doing her job as the local reporter, and frankly, even though this case is awful, it's a sweetheart assignment for a reporter. I said as much to Bertie in the politest way I could manage. Bertie smiled at me and reached out and squeezed my forearm.

"You're a good girl," she said sincerely. "You keep being that."

"*Oh Bertie,*" I thought. "*If only you knew.*"

CHAPTER NINE

Anais was sitting on my bed watching television when I returned to the hotel after leaving the Cogar's to their cleaning.

"Ana!" I said, surprised to see her stretched out and relaxing. It wasn't something I saw much of with Anais. Her showing up without planning it ahead of time was almost unheard of for my hyper-organized friend.

I dropped my bag and walked towards her to hug her but stopped short when she didn't acknowledge me or get up from the bed.

"I'm glad that you responded to this form better," she said in a sultry voice that was alien coming out of her mouth.

"You?" I whispered.

"The cake girl was not my favorite form," she said, tossing the TV remote to the side and looking up at me finally.

I took a step back and put a hand to the gash on my stomach defensively.

"I thought I'd just drop in for a little visit," Grenadine said, swinging Ana's short, shapely legs off of my bed. "Where is that mutt of yours?" she asked.

I stared at her, confused. I didn't have a dog.

"That mongrel you were screwing," she said to me, rolling her eyes in annoyance at my stupidity.

"Work," I replied, continuing my backwards walk towards the door. I had every intention of opening that door and running like hell for my car.

"I think not," Grenadine said, getting up and rushing to me. She grabbed me painfully by my upper arms and threw me across the room and onto my bed.

"I'm going to start taking offense at the way you keep greeting me, Christina." Grenadine said, sprawling out on the bed next to me. She scooched close to me so that our noses were almost touching. "Why don't you like me?"

Of all the things that creature had said to me, this was by far the scariest. I started to realize that Grenadine was something that had been around for so long, was so old, that it had lost its damned mind. I was lying in bed with a deranged fairy.

"You need to fix your pronouns when thinking of me, Christina," Grenadine said. "I am female. You can think of me as one."

That reading my mind stuff made it hard for me to get my thoughts together enough to interact with the thing. With *her*.

"His name is Terry," I said, deciding to return to where the conversation veered when she threw me across the room.

"I'm still thinking about the favor I'm going to bestow upon you," Grenadine said, ignoring me. "It used to be easy. A milking cow, a bag of grain seeds that would yield greatly no matter what, or a blessing promising many strong sons. But now, I'm a bit lost in the times. It's going to take thought on my part and that's not something that I've always been willing to do for your type."

She reached out and poked at the gash on my stomach. I flinched and went to cover the wound with my hands, but she pressed her nose against mine. Her nose was as hard and unmoving as a stone wall and she was slowly applying more pressure with every second. Her hand found the gash and she stabbed a finger onto it, making me yelp. She pressed her nose into mine harder. I wanted to close my eyes and shut out the vision of a green-eyed Anais, but something told me that showing too much weakness to this creature would be my undoing. I kept my eyes open as wide as I could and stared into those eyes like my life depended on it. It probably did. Luckily my eyes started to water, and my vision blurred. She pushed harder on the gash on my stomach. I didn't make a noise. She pushed harder with her nose on mine. I waited in silence for the sound of the cartilage in my nose to give and break.

Then she was gone.

I gasped and sat up. When I realized that she really was gone, I flopped back onto the bed and cried for a little bit. I was scared. I was stressed. I was really confused. I needed to release some stress and I wasn't set to meet Terry until after five and it was only two. Crying helped a little.

When I'd regained some of my composure, I checked on the status of my nose. She'd smashed it, but there was no damage done. The gash on my stomach had been reopened and was seeping red blood all over my thankfully black blouse. I got up and put some anti-bacterial cream on the gash. I'd seen those talons and they didn't look very clean and the last thing I needed was some sort of fairy germ infection. I put on a T-shirt and went to the hotel's gym to get my footsteps in. I shut the world out with music coming from my phone and through some ear buds. I got to 12,000 steps and felt much less stressed and much readier to see if I could resolve this situation without having to compromise my ability to do my job.

I showered and made sure that I smelled nice before I sat down at my laptop to update Anais (*my Anais*) of the progress that I had gotten that day and informed her that hopefully the interview that I had scheduled for the next day would yield enough for me to write up the second installment for our site. Then I opened up my favorite search engine and started doing some research on fairies.

I don't know why I waited so long to do that search except that I am very good at compartmentalizing my life. How else could I have lived with Isaac for months without really seeing the signs that he was cheating? I had to walk in on him mid-hump with someone else in the bed we shared. I'm not the sharpest tack in the box. At least I come around sooner or later, and I was glad at first that my search had millions upon millions of hits related to fairies.

Man, there were some weird hits for that search. Just weird. And not at all helpful to me.

There was a cable TV show that I loved with all of my little fan girl heart. Never mind the name or the premise, but in this show, sometimes research was needed for a neat and tidy resolution to the problem at the end. It always amazed and enraged me at how easily information on some of the most antiquated or esoteric lore could be found in a short amount of time. The very centuries-old book that they needed was always within reach, the internet always yielded the perfect answer. It's all bullshit and not at all fair. Real research takes hours, days, weeks and so on. The show was great, don't get me wrong, but that detail took me out of the story.

As I sorted through stupid mass market fairy garden decorations and Tinkerbell porn, I wished that the internet was filled less with dreams and fetishes and more with that crazy off the grid stuff like in that TV show. Really. In that one afternoon, I saw more than enough gossamer-laden tiny ladies with fully exposed labia.

Finally, I found a page that seemed to be talking about the types of fairies that Grenadine would have called family. It was the type of poorly written website that would have popped up in the early 2000s that had a loudly colored background and the text was white, you had to highlight it in order to be able to read it. What I learned from this antique-by-internet-standards site was that people rarely took a fairy on and put more effort into showing them tribute than anything. They liked cakes. That explained where my other Stripey Cake had gone. Grenadine thought it was for her. There was also some talk about fairies being nocturnal, but I knew that wasn't true because Grenadine was out and about with me in midday on more than one occasion. I saw the rumor that fairies were OCD and if you threw a handful of salt or sugar on the floor, they'd have to stop what they were doing to count all of the crystals. To me, that sounded entirely too stupid to be true, and making a mess on the floor would bother me, even if it didn't bother the fairy.

It appeared that my only options with Grenadine were to do what I could to keep her happy and wait and see what she decided with what to favor me. I really hoped it wouldn't be a head on a platter or anything like that.

Later that night. I was naked in bed next to Terry and filing down a broken nail. He was watching some sort of reality show on the television. I'd discovered that Terry was much more comfortable having sex in the missionary position. He was a little boring, but he was good looking and I was having a good time having sex with him even if it did make me think that it was how my grandparents did it.

"So, are you keeping Stephanie updated on what you're finding out?" Terry asked me suddenly, startling me.

"I didn't realize that we were best buds," I said, keeping my attention on my ragged nail.

"You told her you'd keep in touch," Terry said sternly, turning to me.

I looked over at him and frowned. He stared back at me for a moment and then looked back to the TV.

"I think that she thought that she was going to get something from this. I mean, she helped you, don't you think you ought to help her?" he said.

"With what?" I asked, annoyed. "It was *her* article in the newspaper that brought me here. I'm interviewing people that she's already talked to. What is it that she wants from me?"

Terry kept looking steadily at the TV, the muscles on the side of his face flexing as he clenched and unclenched his deliciously square jaw. He was struggling with something, so I sat up and turned to him, maneuvering myself so that I was straddling him and looking into his face.

"I don't like games," I said simply. "So, what's up?"

He kept his eyes off of mine and tried to move his head away, but I had a good grip on the back of his neck and it was easy to keep swinging my own head around so that I was always in his line of site.

"This isn't me," he said finally.

"Huh?" I asked with extreme intelligence, as one usually does when using such a complicated word.

"I'm not a person who uses other people." He finally locked eyes with me. His hands buried themselves in my hair as he gripped both sides of my head. "I like you. I really do, and I really like this little thing we have. You don't ask me questions that I'm not comfortable answering and you're fun to be around. This isn't using. But what she wants me to do is just...I don't know. She's my friend. Has been for a long time, but I really don't like what she wants me to do."

I just stared at him. So many words had just tumbled out of his mouth and not a single one of them answered my question.

"She thinks that she can get a book deal out of this case eventually and she wants to use what you've found out to add to her data," he said quickly, like he was confessing to a major crime.

"So?" I said back.

He looked at me like I was dense.

"She can use the files from *Killer Chronicles*. As long as she references the site, that's totally acceptable," I said.

"No." Terry said, pulling my hips closer to him and wrapping his arms around my waist. "She wants me to tell her things that I'm supposed to get out of you while we're together so that she can get them published before you. She wants it to look like she's doing all of the work and you're stealing from her."

I sat back, leaning away from him and scrutinized his face.

"You *had* to have heard her wrong," I said. "That's just entirely too evil to be real life."

"She's constantly texting me and calling me. She's badgering me to try to get you talking about it after sex, like pillow talk. She's actually trying to dictate to me how I should open the topic of conversation. I don't know what to say to her. I don't want to get her mad at me, but I don't feel good about using someone like that, especially someone who trusts me enough to go to bed with me."

I could tell that Terry was extremely relieved to be able to confide in someone about this. It was something that was really weighing on him. I kissed him lightly and wiggled my hips into him playfully.

"Just blame it on me," I said to him. "Tell her I refuse to talk work in bed. That way, you won't look like you're short-changing your friend and I won't have to worry about her making me look like a hack."

"She's really persistent," he said. I could tell that my hips were getting the bigger portion of his attention because his pupils were dilated, and he was intently watching my breasts.

"Let her be," I said softly. "I'm not hurting anybody, and neither are you. You just keep telling her little white lies making me sound evasive and she'll have to get off of her ass and do her own damned work."

"You think it will be that easy?" he asked, taking one of my nipples into his mouth.

"I'm not going to be here much longer," I said breathily, leaning back, really angling my hips onto him, feeling his eagerness pushing against me through the bed sheet.

"That's such a shame," he said, getting on his knees and pushing me back. He was getting us back into the missionary position. Again.

I slid onto my stomach instead and angled myself onto all fours. I turned and saw that he had paused, trying to figure out what I was doing. I stretched out and got a condom from the box that I had gotten from the convenience store next to the hotel and handed him one. He knew better than to argue and rolled it on quickly. He then looked at me again, at a loss. I don't understand how; my business was pointed right at him.

"On your knees like that," I guided him. "Grab my hips with your hands. Yeah, like that. Now I'll just move back and you'll slide right in."

"Jesus God!" he exclaimed as I backed onto him. I couldn't help but laugh but laughing caused me to clench and I sort of...well I "spit" him out. This caused him to emit a surprised squawk that caused me to laugh harder.

We eventually got back on track and I was pleased that this was a position that Terry could manage without being awkward, which said to me that he didn't enjoy a submissive sexual position.

People who prefer one over the other and don't spread out seem to have issues understanding that sex should be safe, consensual, fun and not some sort of deep experience that moves heaven and earth. It's just a fuck. But he was a temporary distraction, so I went with it and got out of it what I could. It was good, it's not like he bored me to tears or anything, he just wasn't the type of guy that I wanted to do that with in a long-term committed thing.

When he collapsed onto my back, panting and thanking God, I squirmed out from under him and went to take another shower. When I came out, hair wrapped in a towel and a fluffy terry cloth robe hiding my body, I saw that Terry had dressed and made the bed and was back to watching television. I smiled at him, completely relaxed, and started to gather clean clothes for myself, making a mental note to locate a laundromat to get my other stuff clean.

"Did you mean what you said?" Terry asked me.

"I just said a lot of things," I said. I talk a lot during sex.

"About telling Stephanie that you won't talk to me. About blaming my inability to deliver to her what she wants on you," he said.

"Sure," I said.

"It's going to make her really angry," he said fretfully.

"You know something that I just noticed about you?" I asked.

"What's that?" he asked, looking nervous.

"You don't cuss," I said. It was true, I hadn't heard even so much as a "shit" slip out of his mouth.

He actually blushed.

"My mom doesn't like potty mouths," he answered sheepishly.

"Well neither did mine, but once I hit, like 16, there really wasn't much she could do about it at that point," I said, smiling at him.

"I don't want to be unbecoming or crass," he answered softly. I took a little bit of offense to that but decided that it wasn't worth it to tell him so and continued dressing myself.

"She's going to start bothering you if I tell her you won't talk to me," Terry said, opening that tired old subject again. I sighed heavily and started putting on my shoes, turning my back to him.

"Christina," he said, trying to nudge me to respond.

"Terry!" I said, saying it louder than I meant (that crass and unbecoming comment was still pissing me off). "Stephanie can kiss my fucking ass if she thinks that I'm going to just hand over all of the stuff that I'm gathering on my own. If she had even a shred of gumption to her, she could be doing exactly what I'm doing. OR she could use my findings as reference material and offer me compensation for the help. Otherwise, I am not worried about her being pushy or manipulative. I'm only staying here two, maybe three days longer and then I'm out of here and she will no longer be a problem to me. Okay? Can we drop this? I'm not concerned!"

"She can play dirty," he said softly, shaking his head at me in disappointment.

"Let her," I said. "I'm hungry and would love a big deli sandwich. Is there a Quizno's or a Subway around here?"

Terry felt his defeat and nodded.

With a nutty fairy bothering me, an overly ambitious reporter didn't even show up on my radar of things to freak out over. Ms. D'Agostino could feel free to fuck right off.

CHAPTER TEN

I was feeling like a bit of an ass the next morning. Terry hadn't been able to get away from me fast enough after we'd gotten a couple of subs for dinner and I knew that it was because of my unnecessary outburst. I went and got bagels, doughnuts, coffee, and even a coffee cake and took it to the police station. When I sashayed in, Terry saw me loaded down with bags and steaming cups of coffee and smiled so big that I was certain that his face was going to crack.

Once he'd been filled to the brim with complex carbs and sugars and had had enough caffeine to wake the dead, I sat on the edge of his small press board desk and smiled down at him.

"Uh oh," he said, chuckling softly. "Women only smile at me like that when they want something."

"Hey, fair trade!" I said, throwing my hands up defensively and wearing my best and brightest smile. "I brought food as an apology and I intend to continue the apology tonight."

"But…" Terry said, waving a hand for me to continue.

"No 'but'," I said contrarily. "I'm just also here in a professional capacity, that's all. I wanted to make sure you were good and buttered up for tonight, not for this."

"Okay. *but*…" Terry said again. I laughed and put my foot into his crotch, gently using the pointed toe of my dressy shoe to prod him where he lives. He jerked and pushed my foot away quickly, looking to see if we'd been caught, his face as red as an apple. I laughed carelessly and sat in the hard little chair across from his desk, folding my hands in my lap primly.

"I'd like to see that note that was found in room eight at the Green Hills Motel," I said simply.

"The state police or the FBI took it, I think," Terry said, scratching his chin and jumping up from his desk and going to a wall of files.

The office was a large room occupied by about ten desks and every wall was covered with open shelves of files and boxes. It was a mess and not a way that I would choose to organize so much information, but Terry seemed to have a handle on where everything was located.

He came back to his desk with a fat manila folder and put it down gently. He opened it and carefully turned the pages over until he found what he wanted, and he handed it over to me. I looked around at the other busy people munching happily on the food that I brought in and took the paper. It was the account of the maid from Green Hills and attached to the sheet with a paperclip was a fat envelope containing several different photographs including some of the letter that Katherine had told me about.

Katherine had described the note perfectly from what I could see. The handwriting was abysmal and looked like it had been written with the left hand instead of the right, or vice versa. I couldn't really see much from the pictures about what exactly the writing surface was. Was it old nasty paper? Was it leather? If so, was it Matthew Hart leather? Was this Grenadine's handwriting? Would that matter to my work?

I sighed loudly and started taking some notes on a notepad that I kept in my bag. I usually prefer to take my notes digitally, but my thoughts tend to be more linear if I actually write them out, and this story was too easy to get screwed up. By this point I knew that I had to pretend to be ignorant of who was committing these murders and keep writing as if the assumption was that it was a perfectly mortal human being who had severe rage issues. I started gabbing at Terry to keep him from noticing my agitation.

"It's odd that you all don't do more digital data input. Like, it's weird that you have all of these open files just stashed everywhere. A fire would wipe out your whole system, or a crazy person with a gun and a big van could just take it, right?" I rambled.

"We do input into a secure database that is housed off of the premises," Terry said warmly. "Honestly, the paper part is for the older fellas who aren't very tech savvy and there are hard-copy things that are easier to handle rather than the cold stuff on a computer screen. You can handle and hold those photos and get really close looks whereas the ones that were scanned into the database just don't have the hard cold *evidence* feel to them."

I smiled at him, liking his answer. He busied himself while I finished making notes. He had quietly moved the file back to its place in the wall. I shouldn't have been looking at some of it and he was doing me a big favor by helping. A small part of me whispered in the back of my brain that he might tell Stephanie what I had gathered that day. I didn't fret over it because if she had failed to get at that information at that point, well, she was shitty at her job and was leaning too hard on being helped. Not my problem.

I left not long after, giving Terry a kiss on the cheek and a covert pat on the ass on my way out. I had an appointment at a McDonald's to interview Bridget Maditz, the girlfriend of the guy I was calling The Soap Victim, Martin Hamrick. I had many questions for Ms. Maditz, especially in light of what Grenadine had told me about her personal bar of Martin soap. How I was going to get any details out of her concerning that was beyond me. I had spent hours thinking about it and couldn't get around the fact that the murderer confided in me about the soap and unless I told Ms. Maditz that, I was going to have to hope for the unlikely.

I came upon Bridget Maditz sitting in a booth that was decorated to resemble a somber café as opposed to the brightly colored plastic looking restaurants of my youth. She was sipping a large, iced coffee and looking around her nervously, her eyes darting about the restaurant. She had the appearance of a frazzled pink Muppet with her frizzy orange hair and Winnie the Pooh tank top. I gave her a small wave with a warm smile on my face and went to the register to order a Diet Coke. When I had my drink, I made my way to her booth. She watched me approach uncomfortably and fidgeted, making the vinyl seat make embarrassing sounds under her.

"Ms. Maditz," I said as congenially as I could manage. "Thank you so much for meeting me. Can I get you anything to eat? It is nearly lunch time."

I had to offer. It made me look generous and friendly. I hoped she'd say no. I was still full from all of the confections at the police station and I didn't want to have to skip dinner in order to maintain my calorie limit.

"No thank you," she said softly. She had a sweet, high pitched voice.

"Alright then, but you let me know if that changes, okay? I'll try not to take up too much of your time. Now let me begin this by saying how very sorry I am for your loss. I can't imagine how hard it has been on you losing someone so close to you. You have my sympathies," I said, observing the formalities as an icebreaker.

She nodded simply, lowering her eyes and taking an awkward drink of her beverage. I noticed that her fingernails were short and clean and I felt myself sink back into the booth, relaxing more by the second.

I went through my usual spiel with getting her permission to record the interview and take her photograph. She declined the photograph, but agreed to the voice recorder, so when my small voice recorder was sitting atop the table between us, I took out my notebook with prepared questions and pulled out a pencil.

"Can you tell me about how you found out about what happened to Martin?" I asked.

"The police came to my door. They told me that he had checked into a motel and they'd found his clothes and a note that made them believe that something happened to him. They didn't know about the soap for sure yet and they didn't say nothing to me about it. When they knew for sure about the soap, they came and gave me their condolences," she answered. I could tell that she had told that story before by the way her voice had gone monotone.

"How long had he been missing before the police came to you the first time?" I asked.

"Not long enough for me to really start worrying about him," Bridget answered coolly.

"Can you please try to elaborate?" I asked.

"The man was usually feet up in a bottle if you know what I mean. He'd go on benders and crash on couches or sleep in his car. It wasn't weird for him not to come home at night. Him going to a motel? That was weird. He was a cheap bastard and never spent money on nothing except Wild Turkey and Bud." She got a little heated there at the end. I decided to prod about the motel.

"Were you told for certain whether or not he had someone with him when he checked into the motel?" I asked.

"No. I mean, he had to either have had someone with him or was going to meet someone. Son of a bitch. He had more shortcomings than a person ought to, but I never pegged him for a cheater," she said angrily.

I nodded sympathetically. And I meant it. It's not fun to be blindsided like that.

She leaned forward, elbows on the table and whispered to me.

"He was a bad man," she breathed. "He would get in the drink and beat me. And sometimes he made me do sex things that were bad."

I leaned forward to meet her, a look of feigned concern on my face.

"Like what?" I whispered back.

She looked down for a minute, thinking about whether or not to tell me.

"He'd make me lay down naked in the bathtub and he'd..." she paused.

Just say it, I thought, knowing what was coming.

"He'd go to the bathroom all over me," she said, her eyes lowered and shame sending a flame of red creeping up her neck and into her face.

I reached out and patted her hand, sincerely feeling sorry for her.

"That must have been horrible," I said.

"It was," she answered. "He would aim for my face and try to get me to open my mouth. But it was awful. It would get in my eyes and go up my nose and it's just a smell that would be inside of my head for hours after."

I grimaced. My head would not be able to take that kind of torture. I'd bathe in bleach and kill the guy in his sleep.

"You'd need a pretty strong soap for that," I blurted. I didn't mean to say it and I was certain that she wouldn't suspect that I knew anything, but I knew better than to blurt. Interviewers do not blurt.

"Yeah," she said, smiling sideways and looking uncomfortable. "Any soap will do, though."

"Well I think that that is all that I need from you Ms. Maditz," I said, clicking the voice recorder off. "I'd like to thank you again for giving me your time and I truly am sorry for your loss even though, if you'll excuse me for saying this, it sounds like life is looking a bit brighter for you now that it's all over."

"It's sad that that's the case," she said, getting up from the booth. "But it is. Life will be better for me now."

She smiled at me and turned and walked out of the McDonald's. I watched her go, nodding in agreement. After talking to Bridget Maditz, I was glad that Martin Hamrick had died. Usually, I was pretty good at maintaining a sense of detachment from the crimes that I wrote about. Every once in a while, one would get under my skin and I would feel a deep pain and sympathy for the victim and their families that it would form a hard ball in my gut and Anais would have to take over for a while. I didn't know much about Martin Hamrick, and being someone who profiles murderers, it's my job to look at all of the angles of the human psyche to find reasons for this and that. For Martin Hamrick, I had no interest in that and only felt a sense of relief that the world was free of one more piss-poor excuse for a human being.

CHAPTER ELEVEN

Why I drove to Grenadine's pond, I have no idea. I was feeling tense and I didn't want to be around any people. Aside from my hotel room, it was the most peaceful place that I could think of. I stayed in my car and ate a Fudge Mound, not willing to share anything with the batty fairy who lived...in the water? In a dimension accessed by the water? I didn't know.

As I sat in my car, windows closed tightly and the air conditioner keeping me cool, I saw someone walking among the vegetation in my rearview mirror. Startled, I spun in my seat and saw Stephanie approaching my car. She was dressed in a sharply pressed pair of brown slacks and a maroon blouse that offset her olive complexion in a very becoming way.

She came up to my passenger side door and made a gesture with her hand like she was pulling up one of those old-style car door locks. I hit the button to unlock the door and she got in, sighing heavily as she settled in and slammed the door.

"You said you'd stay in touch," she said lightly.

"I've been busy," I said, frowning at her and leaning away, not sure what to expect.

"Busy fucking Terry," she said. "Do you do this on all of your case files?"

I rolled my eyes and sat back heavily into my seat. Terry's chattiness was a quirk that I did not appreciate in the least.

"I sort of thought you'd like to cooperate with me on this," she said. "I've been happy to share what I know and since things are moving slowly, I would have appreciated a little wheel greasing from you."

"Yeah, Terry told me that you were trying to get him to get some stuff out of me," I said. I could use Terry's big mouth to my advantage too. "I gab *during* sex, Stephanie, not after."

I tried not to laugh at the amazing reaction that I got out of Stephanie. Her mouth was hanging open and her eyes were wide. Her mouth started working, trying to find something to say and I just sat staring back at her, biting the inside of my cheek. She surprised me when she reached behind my seat and grabbed my bag and jumped out of my car with it. I scurried after her, but she was running as hard as she could toward the pond. She turned and looked back at me and then twisted her upper body and swung as hard as she could and threw my bag at the pond. I screamed at her and watched helplessly as the bag that held all of my notes and the voice recorder headed for the serene brown water.

My bag didn't hit the water. It didn't hit anything. I watched it soar towards a watery death, and then Grenadine was standing next to me, handing my bag back to me. I screamed and jumped to the side, falling to the ground with a thud. The noise (and lack of a splash from my bag) caused Stephanie to spin to face me.

"That wasn't nice, you petty thing," Grenadine said to Stephanie. She was back in her Nummy Nellie form, the sunny blue bonnet crowning her head.

"No," I said from the ground. "Go away! Don't do this!"

"Shut up," Grenadine snapped at me.

"What the hell?" Stephanie said, staying by the edge of the pond.

"Stephanie D'Agostino," Grenadine purred. "Why are you bullying Christina Cunningham? And why are you throwing things at my nice clean pond?"

Instinct had me scrambling on my back away from the little girl who was advancing towards Stephanie. I was the only human that I knew of who had interacted with Grenadine in modern times who lived to tell the tale. And seeing how she was looking at Stephanie, I was worried that that trend was going to continue.

"Tsk tsk," Grenadine said to Stephanie, shaking her head. "What a messy person you are, Stephanie."

Grenadine turned to me and smiled. Her grayish-green teeth scared me as bad as her gross dirty talons. Reading my mind, Grenadine barked a laugh and put a demure hand over her mouth.

"She was planning on surprising Terry at work today," Grenadine said to me. "She was going to seduce him. She was going to try to use sex to get answers out of him. She's done it before. Terry is convinced that they are friends, but any time he feels conflicted about giving in to her demands, this woman uses sex to get it out of him."

I looked at Stephanie and she was again wearing her gape-mouthed face of shock, staring at the little girl in the blue and white checkered dress.

"Honestly, Christina, I don't know why you bother with that idiot," Grenadine said, picking on Terry again.

Grenadine ran to Stephanie. Stephanie put her hands out before her and almost fell back into the pond. Grenadine had stopped right in front of Stephanie and was looking up into her face. She turned to me and smiled her decaying grin at me again.

"Would you like to see my stew pot, my little investigator?" she asked me.

"No," I said, realizing I had been holding my breath, and I started panting to try to get oxygen going through me again.

"It's a lovely stew pot, Christina," Grenadine said. She turned and grabbed Stephanie by one of her wrists. Stephanie yipped in pain and tried to pull away. Grenadine pulled Stephanie down to face level and slapped Stephanie. Still holding Stephanie's wrist, Grenadine turned and started walking the ten or so yards back to where I was lying.

"I haven't had a guest for dinner in an age," Grenadine said. When she reached me, she touched one of her taloned fingers to the tip of my nose.

I wasn't sprawled out on a mossy piece of land by the pond anymore. I was seated at a honey-colored heavy wood table looking at an enormous blazing fireplace. I jumped and made a noise that sounded something like when you step on a cat.

I looked at my surroundings. I was in some sort of rustic dwelling with rough but clean stone floors and the walls had the same warm, honey-colored wood as the table. The fireplace was enormous. I could have walked into it standing completely upright and maybe even parked my small car inside of it. I recognized the smell of the place as the way Grenadine always smelled; wood smoke, green leaves, and cool clean air. It was warm and cozy and completely freaking delightful.

And of course, hanging from a hook, sitting just askew of the roaring fire was an enormous, shining brass stew pot. It wasn't the rough black that I was expecting and seeing that glowing brass made me think of Christmas. Everything here managed to be simple, yet grand all at once.

I noticed Stephanie hanging by her hands from the ceiling in the corner farthest from the fireplace. The place sort of lost its charm then.

I got up as quietly as I could from the heavy wooden chair I was inexplicably plopped onto and made my way to Stephanie, a finger over my mouth gesturing for her to be quiet. Her face had gone an alarming shade of white and her eyes were darting all over the room in panic. I did a quick look around to make sure we were alone and then I reached up to try and get her hands free. She had her hands bound with what looked like a thin, gold-thread rope that was hung over a shiny brass hook hanging from the ceiling. I also noticed that there was a rough, heavy cloth sitting beneath Stephanie's feet and I began to panic when I thought of the enormous brass stew pot.

"Just hold still and be as quiet as you can," I whispered up into Stephanie's face. She nodded quickly and whimpered.

I spun around and searched the room for something to cut the rope and I saw nothing. My mind raced, and I got an idea. I turned to Stephanie and got into her face again so that I could whisper closely and know that she was hearing me.

"I'm going to climb you," I said to her. "I need to get a little bit higher to pull the rope tying your hands off of the hook up there and then we'll get the fuck out of here, okay?"

Stephanie looked up at the hook and then looked down at me, scared out of her mind. That made two of us.

"Okay," she said. "Please hurry."

I reached up and put my hands on her shoulders and lifted myself so that I could wrap my legs around her waist. I went a little too high and my thighs ended up gripping her ribs. She grunted and gasped from the squeezing, but I kept with it because getting her out of there was more important than making sure that she could breathe easier for a few seconds. I squeezed tight with my thighs and moved myself up so that I could slip the rope off of the hook, but it was too tight and wouldn't move up quite enough. I cursed my stupidity and got down. Stephanie gasped as quietly as she could manage.

"I'm sorry, that was a really stupid idea," I breathed at her. "I'm going to bring one of those chairs over here and you're going to climb onto it and free your own hands, okay?"

"Yeah, okay. We should have done that first," she said.

I ran to the table and tried to pick up one of the heavy wooden chairs, but it slipped from my grip and slammed onto the stone floor. I looked around frantically and tried again, struggling with the size and weight of the thing the whole way to Stephanie. I finally got it to her and she stepped up onto it and reached up to slip the rope off of the hook. I watched her jerk her hands once, twice, three times, each jerk getting more frantic.

"What?" I asked.

"It won't come off!" she said.

"Just pull the loop off of the hook!" I said to her.

"What the fuck do you think I'm doing?" she spat down at me. "It gets tighter or something the closer it gets to the end of the hook and it won't come off."

"Okay, okay, let me look!" I said, climbing onto the chair with her and trying to get a look.

She was right. Whatever knot that had tied the thin, ribbon-like rope was designed to get tighter the more you pulled on it and by the time it had started sliding up the curve of the hook, it was too tight to move any further.

"It's not a knot that makes it do that," I heard Grenadine's smooth voice say from behind me.

I spun around and was completely thrown off by what I saw. It wasn't Nummy Nellie, nor was it Anais. It was Grenadine. Her real skin. And even though her coloring was not something you'd normally see on a human, she wasn't as nasty as I expected she would be. She was actually sort of beautiful.

Yeah, her skin was a sickly gray color, and when seen on only one body part when surrounded by a typically peachy human skin tone, it looked gross. But when it is the main color it is much easier to digest. Her fingers all had those nasty talons on them, but here on her home turf, they looked glossy, sort of like how I imagined a dragon's talons would look. Her hair was brown, mousey brown, but it was long and wavy, and she wore it in a loose braid down her back with little white flowers woven into the plait. Her eyes were black. Totally all one color. No iris, no pupils, no white part. All black. She was wearing a sort of shift that was the color of tree bark, but it looked soft and it looked clean.

"Don't think that anything here is even remotely human," Grenadine said, smiling at me. "You can't handle a rope woven by a fairy. What makes you think it would be that easy for you?" Her grin widened.

Okay, the teeth thing was still there, and she stopped being beautiful when she smiled. She looked like the scary crazy thing with the stew pot of horrors I didn't want to know about. Apparently, Stephanie agreed with my views on that and she started crying at the sight of that hideous smile.

Grenadine turned away from the sobbing Stephanie to return the enormous, heavy chair to its spot at the table. She did it with one hand. When it was back in place, she patted the seat, beckoning me. I gave a long look at Stephanie, thinking as fast as I could of a way to get us both out of this.

"Stop it and come sit," Grenadine said to me harshly. "You're not even in your own world anymore, so let it go."

I walked to the chair with the sound of Stephanie's sobbing ringing in my ears.

"No, don't leave me up here!" Stephanie said to my back.

I looked at Grenadine and a thought hit me.

"Let her go," I said. "Let this be the favor that you owe me."

The next thing I knew, I was leaning over that heavy table and one side of my face really, really hurt. I stood up straight and looked at Grenadine, who was standing right next to me, her fist still clenched from where she had clocked me. She reached out one of her taloned hands and gripped my jaw roughly.

"You don't get to decide the favor with which I will grace you, you insect!" she growled into my face. "Now sit down and be quiet! Maybe you'll learn something, and I won't have to write off your entire race as a waste to the world."

I sat down like a good little listener. Grenadine nodded down at me and then walked to Stephanie. She pulled a scary looking hooked knife out of a hidden pocket in her shift and held it up to the light, making sure that Stephanie was getting a good look. Stephanie's eyes were wide, and her mouth was closed tight and turned down.

"Stephanie D'Agostino," Grenadine practically purred at Stephanie. "You are a bad and manipulative woman. You had terrible parents who put you down as a child and you grew up to become a vicious and ambitious creature that cares little for the people you use as long as the means meet your own selfish end. You were going to hurt my little pet over there," Grenadine pointed the knife at me, "and you have badly used that poor, wet rag that you both copulate with on occasion. Stephanie D'Agostino, as a being superior to yourself, I deem you unworthy of my universe and choose instead to add you to my stew pot." Grenadine turned and pointed her knife now at the gleaming brass pot.

"Let me go. I'm not a bad person! I donate to charities! I take care of my parents! I pay their bills!" Stephanie cried out.

Grenadine started slowly unbuttoning Stephanie's blouse, revealing the luscious skin and black, lace bra beneath. Next came the button of the snappy brown slacks that slid down her lovely round thighs as they fell to her ankles.

"You donate to charities so that you can write a yearly column wherein you brag about said charitable giving. The bills you say you pay for your parents are their medical care and home nurses so that you don't have to bother visiting them." Grenadine slid the knife seductively along the delicate skin of Stephanie's ribs. "I've certainly seen worse humans, but you can't be bothered to strive for a better version of yourself. I'm going to put those expensively manicured hands of yours in a box and mail them to one of those charities you liked to brag about donating to. If you'd actually exercised a human heart instead of your newspaper's expense account, you'd perhaps have actually improved someone's life by being a part of it."

Before either Stephanie or I could react, Grenadine buried that curved knife into Stephanie's lower stomach and drove it up, curly guts and shining wet innards spilling from the gash. The guts started to unravel, and they fell to the cloth on the floor with a wet thud, but the rest of Stephanie's organs stayed hanging in a mass just inside of the wound.

Stephanie was trying to scream, but with her stomach muscles ripped apart and her innards poking out of the long gash going down the length of her torso, the most she could manage were choking gasps and grunts. Her eyes were bulging from their sockets, twirling about and looking everywhere, but apparently seeing nothing.

My hands had flown up to my mouth and I wished they would go to my eyes and cover them, but I couldn't seem to look away from the slowly spilling intestines. The wet sound of them moving out of her body was so exaggerated that it sounded like a bad sound effect in a low-budget horror movie and the blood was such a bright red that it almost didn't seem real. Wet slithering, Stephanie's gasping and grunting, the ripping sound of the knife doing its work, it was a series of noises that I would have been happy to have never heard in all of my life.

I suddenly registered that I was crawling underneath of that massive table with my hands over my head and my eyes squeezed shut. I shut out the sounds as much as I could, but some splats and crunches still came through. It also didn't help that Grenadine started dictating to me her actions once I stopped being a willing spectator. There was no escape. No happy place.

"Now we have to cut the tissues that are keeping everything attached to the body so that they all spill out. I won't use these in the stew, but there's a creature that lives not far from here who appreciates organ meat heartily. Oops, I popped the stomach. *Woo*, that's a smell, isn't it, Christina? (God awful fucking smell when she popped that stomach.) Now we just reach up inside of the ribcage and cut out the heart and lungs. Ooh, there she goes, she's dead now. Farewell, Stephanie! I hope you make a better stew than a human being."

I was singing to myself, a sort of ingrained way of self-soothing. It was the Nummy Nellie jingle again.

"A pack of love, a pack of happy," I choked out. "Share a cake and make it snappy."

"NUMMY NELLIEEEEEEES IS LOVE FOR THE BELLY!" Grenadine finished for me.

I stopped singing.

"You're being childish, Christina," Grenadine said to me. "You like to think that you've toughened up to stuff like this. I know you've seen some pretty grisly crime photos, how is this so much different?"

"Because I can smell her blood and guts!" I yelled from under the table.

"Hmm, yes, the sense of smell is the one most tied to memory, isn't it? Oh well. Your line of work needs a level of reverence to it for it to be done well. Now, I'm not accusing you of being someone who sensationalizes murderers like some of your critics, but I do think that you try to protect yourself from the ugliness of it all by distancing yourself from the pain that your fellow humans have suffered and that's a useless tactic, Christina. Ugliness, in its contrast to beauty, enhances beauty. If it didn't storm every now and then, how could you really appreciate a sunny day? Look at this, Christina. Look at it so that you can look at living people walk down the street and see their life and see it for the precious thing it is."

I was shaking my head under the table, eyes still closed tightly and hands still over my head when I felt a warm wet hand gently grab one of my wrists and start to pull me up and out from under the table. I couldn't fight the pulling, and I knew better not to at this point. I didn't want to end up in the stew pot.

I was pulled to a standing position and when I opened my eyes, I felt my throat clench shut to hold back the tidal wave of vomit trying to make a prison break.

Stephanie's hair was now tied to the hook hanging from the ceiling, holding her severed head off of the mess on the floor. I stared at Stephanie's dead face longer than I wanted to. In the movies, the face always gets nasty and scuffed, even during a neat decapitation. There's always blood that comes out of the mouth and nose and the eyes go all wonky and crooked, but Stephanie's face was clean and even serene looking. She looked pale, but other than that, she looked asleep. Until, of course, you noticed the neat cut along the neck that liberated her head from her gutted body.

Her body was skinned and cleaned on the floor. Grenadine worked preternaturally fast because both arms had already been cut off and it looked like the meat was being removed and cut into stew-sized cubes. The hands had been cut from the arms and were sitting neat and clean on a separate cloth near the body.

"Yes, I really am going to send those to a charity. Something called the ASPCA, for animals I suppose. If she'd worked those hands in an honest and genuine way, they would be better than the polished things lying cold and dead on that cloth," Grenadine said to me.

I watched her strip the meat off of Stephanie's arms and take the bones to a large bin at the far end of the room. There was a heavy board on top of the bin, but she removed it easily with one hand. I could hear a strange sound coming from the bin. Grenadine put a hand into the bin and scooped out a handful of fat, white squirming maggots. The sound I was hearing was of their disgusting bodies wriggling about and rubbing against each other.

"They're actually very clean," Grenadine said, reading my mind. She gently placed the maggots back into the noisy bin and she put the meatless arm inside.

"They are wonderful at stripping away that excess tissue. I'll roast the bones once they're stripped and make more stock for the stew pot," she said.

I gagged at the thought of maggoty stew broth.

She left me standing there by myself and went out of a door. She returned with a basket full of root vegetables and herbs. She winked at me and started chopping the hearty vegetables from her basket and tossing them into the hot brass pot sitting over her goddamned enormous fire.

"You shouldn't be so upset over this, Christina," Grenadine said to me as her hands flew over the vegetables, the knife in her hand working as an articulated extension, cutting so fast that her movements registered as little more than a blur to my eyes.

"As much as you love to eat meat, you should remember that it came from a creature that was once a living being with a life and habits and a place in the world. Meat comes from life, Stephanie, not the grocery store wrapped in sanitary plastic wrap and Styrofoam trays. To be blind to the slaughter that goes into those meals you love is to rob yourself of the real experience of extinguishing life and taking the remains into yourself. It really is a beautiful thing if you think about it. Nothing should be taboo." Grenadine seemed to have a sense of calm over her as she kept her hands busy. She was the most coherent when she was chatting while having something to work on with her hands.

"I've eaten the flesh of many living things. Birds, large game animals, giants, other fairies, humans, all of it. I think my favorite meat, though, is the flesh of the young. I know some of your kind agree with me. Lamb, veal, suckling pigs. All succulent and tender and just the finest of meats. Back in the times of small villages and human reverence and fear for my kind, I used to be fond of stealing human babes from their sleeping places and roasting them in clay pots. I could never do it as often as I would have liked, as you humans have an unnatural love for your young that only causes undue grief when they die or are taken. A young one fresh from the womb would have been the perfect tribute to me and mine, but you are strange creatures, Christina. Truly strange."

"I want to go," I squeaked out. I didn't want to listen to her talking about roasting babies anymore and I didn't want to watch poor Stephanie being butchered.

I didn't want the warm pleasant smell of the brown liquid in the stew pot in my nose anymore. I didn't want the pleasing smell to cause my stomach to growl anymore.

I didn't want to see the head hanging from a hook by its hair anymore.

"Shall I let you keep her head as a trophy, Christina?" Grenadine asked me, walking to the head and knocking at it lazily so that it swayed back and forth.

"I want to go home," I said, backing away.

"I still owe you something, Christina," Grenadine said to me. "I'll be seeing you."

I fell to my ass in the sandy ground by the pond. I was sitting in front of my car. Stephanie was gone. Grenadine was gone. My bag was sitting neatly next to me.

CHAPTER TWELVE

I drove like hell was at my heels back to my hotel. I ran up to my room and started packing my things, noticing the blood on my arm from where Grenadine had pulled me out from under the table. I took a break from packing to wash the blood away with the hottest water I could stand and the complimentary bar of harsh soap three times. I planned to call Anais on the road to tell her things got too weird for me and that we would have to put this file on the backburner for the time being. I didn't think enough of Terry to really care about telling him I was leaving town and I sincerely hoped that he had enough sense to think little enough of me to not care. I'd miss his thigh-clenchingly handsome face smiling at me, sure, but there were other guys in towns that didn't have fairies with fucking stew pots that would haunt my dreams for the rest of my life. I knew that I could always send an apologetic text later.

I had loaded all of my stuff into the trunk of my car and decided to walk to the front desk to checkout so that I could get some footsteps in. The parking lot was sectioned off into squares and the squares were separated by blocks of manicured shrubbery. I was passing one of these that had a holly tree when I felt a hand grip my shoulder and pull me back. The pull was so hard that I fell on my ass for the umpteenth time that day. I blinked a couple of times and noted the pain in my tailbone and butt when I looked up into the face of a really, really angry Grenadine. I shrank away from the blazing black orbs that she called eyes and heard myself whimper.

You never think of yourself as the type of person that would whimper if you saw something scary, but then something scary is staring at you nose-to-nose and there you go. You're a whimperer and have little inclination at the time to give a damn.

"This will not be happening, Christina," Grenadine growled into my face. I could smell meat on her breath.

"I want to go home," I said, scared out of my mind.

"How would you like for me to go to Parkersburg and grab that mom of yours and make you watch me add her to my stew pot? Or Anais? Have you ever seen someone get raped by the business end of a gutting knife, Christina? Because I could make that happen for you. If you continue to show me this disrespect, I'm going to have to do something to put you in your place." Grenadine, in her Nummy Nellie form, wrapped one of her craggy fingers around the lobe of my right ear. She stroked it gently at first as she stared holes into me, but then I felt one of her talons gouge the top cartilage. I managed a pained squeak, but I knew that if I made a fuss, I'd bring unwanted attention to this situation and it would end badly for the good Samaritan coming to my rescue.

Grenadine pulled her claw out of my ear and licked at it, making a disgusting smacking sound with her lips.

"You taste nice," she said. "I wonder if it's hereditary. Your mom could be my dessert."

"Stop," I said. "What do you want me to do?" I asked. I was prepared to resign myself to the will of this thing in order to protect my mom and Anais.

"You're going to stay put until I can think of what I can do to pay off your tribute," Grenadine said, millimeters from my face. Her lips brushed mine as she spoke.

"Okay," I breathed, moving my head aside to get away from her soft lips and from the terrible sensation of arousal that they brought on in me. To me, I was almost kissing an older-than-time creature from another realm, but to an onlooker it looked like I was being seduced by Nummy Nellie. I'd been walked in on having sex by Anais, I'd been caught picking my nose, but being caught looking like I was being seduced by a snack cake mascot was too much.

"Then you be a good girl and go put your things back in that room, go launder the filth out of your clothes, and do your work as is expected of you," Grenadine said.

Instead of her usual disappearing act, Grenadine actually stood up and backed away from me so that I could stand up. I dusted my pants off and looked down at her.

"Just remember that I'm not done with you yet," she said, smiling up at me. "I'll never be far."

She did her unnerving "now you see me, now you don't" thing and I walked back to my car, climbed into the backseat and fell asleep. I know that sounds like the absolute last thing one would do in a situation where you've had the wits scared out of you, but that was my second run-in with Grenadine that day and the adrenaline rushes and crashes exhausted me. It was weird, I'd been sleeping extremely well since Grenadine first came to me. Sometimes I attributed it to my time with Terry, but it was more likely that it was the stress of trying to maintain a normal façade and work life while also carrying the knowledge that I'd found the murderer I was profiling. She was a murderer I knew that I could never write about if I ever hoped to be taken seriously. And I really hoped to be taken seriously.

I woke up to orange skies and a growling stomach. It was early evening. I had slept for several hours (as I had noticed while packing that time barely moved while I was away in Grenadine's world which helped to explain how she was able to butcher and process her victims with such unbelievable speed) and was sorely in need of some comfort food.

I forced my stiff body out of the backseat of my car and pulled my belongings from the trunk and trudged to my room. After my stuff was deposited, I returned an email and text message to Anais explaining what I had accomplished that day with regards to the file. I had to give myself a minute to remember meeting with Bridget Maditz that morning, but I was able to promise Anais another write-up the next day.

I missed Ana. I wanted to go home to our apartment and sit on our couch with her and talk to her. I wanted to tell her about Grenadine and all of the shit I'd seen, and I wanted her to listen to me with that deep look of empathy that I loved about her and I wanted her to tell me that I did a good job with the interviews. I wanted her to make popcorn and watch trash TV with me and I wanted to hear the familiar sounds of her trying to quietly move about the apartment when she thought I was sleeping. Anais was where home was for me. She was my safe place and I needed her.

When Ana and I had met in college, we had a few of the same classes together, but we really bonded doing work study in the same building. We often pulled shifts together and we found that our personalities complimented each other. All four years of school we were friends and after graduation, she remained someone with whom I maintained close contact. After my relationship with Isaac fell apart and I moved out of our apartment, Ana became more than just my friend, she became my rock. She listened to me without interjecting with her own stories. She assured me that I wasn't to blame for Isaac's cheating and she was the one who got me thinking that casual relationships are a good balm for a bruised soul. It was even Ana's mother's couch that I went to until I found another apartment with a stranger for a roommate. I was working for a second-rate local publication in those days and doing freelance writing for various blogs. When my roommate wanted to move out when our lease renewal came up, it was Ana who took her place and that's when we started *Killer Chronicles*. I quit my penny paper job and put all of my focus on Ana's idea. She's a lot smarter than I am and it was amazing to me to see her do the work to build an idea into something as great as *Killer Chronicles*. She's an amazing woman and she's someone I wish I could be more like.

I considered calling her, but she would know something was up from my voice and she would insist on coming down to be with me. I couldn't have that, so I sucked it up and sent her a perky text telling her I'd be busy for the rest of the night with Terry.

The truth was, I did not want to see Terry. I probably never wanted to see him again. He was a mess and I didn't have room for that. I wanted to be alone and pace my hotel room with bags of fast food littering the bed and fret over my fate without him there.

I was sitting in the Taco Bell drive-thru when he texted me asking what I wanted to do that night. I hit my head on my steering wheel in a nice show of melodrama and thought about what to say. Stephanie was gone. Forever. He'd want to know what happened to her. He might know that she was following me. He might suspect that I did something. I might have looked guilty if I suddenly stopped wanting to see him. I chickened out.

"Sorry, can't tonight," I texted back. "Got a lot of writing and note taking to do. Sorry."

"No problem! There's always tomorrow!" He texted back.

"Yeah right," I said to myself, tossing my phone back into my bag and taking the food from the person at the drive-thru window.

My food accompanied me to a laundromat near my hotel so that I could wash all of my clothes. I'd given up on having a timeline for going home, so I sat on a hideous orange plastic chair from the 1970s and ate chalupas and read nonsense on my cell phone while my clothes were tossed about the enormous machines. Two hours later, I was back in my hotel when my phone dinged at me, alerting me to a text message. I was relieved to see that it was from Anais, but the content of the message did not make me happy.

"Hey, I know you're busy right now, but I've got to address a problem with the name you've picked for your killer out there. I know you've got a thing for alliteration and usually that's fine, except for when you tried to get me to call the site *Killer Kronicles*. I love you, but that was awful Chris. I thought it would be a neat idea, since this is our first hit-by-hit file, if we allowed our readers to name the murderer. I know it amps up the sensationalism, but I've got bills to pay. I've already put the offer up on the forum, and so far, there's been some really good ones on there. Catchy ones. I hope you don't let this one get you down. The work you're doing down there is amazing and we're getting a metric fuckton of hits on the site because of this and that's all because of you. This was your idea and you were right on the button with it, so please don't let something little like the name get to you. I'll let you know my top three favorites tomorrow and we can decide together what the new name will be. Miss you, *mami*."

I sat my phone back on the desk in my room and slumped back on my chair. I wasn't angry, but I was a little hurt. Of course it wasn't Ana's fault and I wasn't really upset with her, I was upset with myself. Why did I have these hang ups that made me so weird? I'd never be seen as a legitimate journalist if I couldn't stop being so neurotic. I liked the Micksburg Mauler. There was a classic feel to it.

"You just use alliteration as a crutch. You get stuck on things that make you feel safe and comfortable and then you beat them into the ground until they no longer serve that purpose," a voice said from my bed.

I yipped and spun around, mistaking the chair at the desk for the swiveling office chair in my home office and I hit my ribs and left breast on the hard curved back of the chair as I spun. I grunted and held my screaming boob and squeezed my eyes shut until the initial flashes of pain subsided to a dull, throbbing ache. When I opened my eyes again, I actually sighed when I saw Nummy Nellie sitting cross-legged on my bed, looking at me.

"Those are sensitive, aren't they?" Grenadine asked me, gesturing to my offended breast.

"If you smash them into a hard chair back, then yes," I said.

"I thought that I'd visit you to let you know that Stephanie D'Agostino's car has been found abandoned near my pond, on that little country road. They'll find her hands in a box by the telephone of the ASPCA tomorrow complete with a nice note. You'll be busy tomorrow, Christina," Grenadine said to me. My stomach knotted. I needed to deny having seen Stephanie at all that day.

"Why are you still in that form?" I asked, a bad mood taking a tight hold of me. "You said you didn't care for this one and I've seen the real you. You're very close to ruining Nummy Nellie for me."

"Don't assume that I do anything for your comfort at this point, Christina," Grenadine said to me, getting off of my bed and rifling through my bag. She pulled a cellophane square out containing a Fudge Mound and opened it, sniffing the heavenly confection before folding the entire thing into her mouth.

"These are marvelous," she said, closing her black eyes and savoring my last Fudge Mound.

"I like them too," I said, wanting to keep her in a chatty mood, hoping she wouldn't flip out and attack me for a third time that day.

"People used to make cakes themselves, but you buy them. Why would your kind unlearn a necessary skill like cooking and baking?" she asked me.

"We didn't," I answered. "Personally, I don't bake or cook simply because I don't want to. I'm busy with other things in my life. But there are a lot of people who cook and bake quite well. We didn't unlearn anything. And those cakes you love? Those aren't even widely considered to be good. They're junk food that isn't even considered a decent dessert."

Grenadine frowned at me and started pacing the room. She was starting to look agitated. I got nervous and considered hiding under the desk until she went away.

"I remember," she said softly. "There used to be honey cakes. They were dense and coarse. They were good, but not as good as this junk food you give me. I remember."

"What happened that you forgot so much?" I ventured, more interested in keeping her talking than anything. I flinched when she turned to me too quickly, but she frowned and started pacing again.

"I don't know," she said. "There used to be a lot of us. Being around my kind, I think, would have kept me from forgetting. But I haven't seen another of my own in a long time. I don't know why. I don't remember."

She was pacing, wringing her little pink hands together. I'd get flashes of her real form every now and then, sort of like whatever glamour she had going on was losing its potency with her agitation. One minute I would be looking at a confused Nummy Nellie and then for just a split second I would be looking at the real Grenadine in her soft brown shift, bare feet stomping on the low-pile carpet of my hotel room.

"There were giants once. I remember that. We hunted them and tricked humans into killing them and then we would take control of their enormous castles. That's why so many tales of my world involve all fairies living in castles. At one time, we did. I don't know what happened to those castles, though. I don't remember. Why don't I live in a castle anymore? Where are the other fairies? How did I end up alone and with no memory?"

I became cognizant of a tremor going on beneath me. It was like when I lived in a small house and the whole house shook when the washing machine was on its spin cycle. The more she paced, the more questions she asked, the more things shook. It never swelled, it never got more violent, and it just stayed a soft, nearly silent tremor.

"Stop that," Grenadine said absently, waving a hand at the air. The tremors stopped.

"What was that?" I asked, worried.

"It was me. I could split this hotel in two if I really concentrated on it. I could end this world with just a thought, Christina," Grenadine said.

I swallowed hard and tried to look at something other than Grenadine. She was talking quietly to herself, barely registering my presence. Maybe in my attempts to remain a calm little cucumber, I had not taken the time to properly let my brain absorb exactly what it was that I was dealing with. I'd thought it, sure. But I hadn't really let it sink in. Grenadine's cheese had slipped right off of her pizza.

"Were you ever considered a deity?" I asked, hoping to get her to stop that damned pacing.

"Yes," she answered. "I was worshiped, and sacrifices were laid out for my service. Oddly, that wasn't my favorite time. I liked it better when humans left little cakes for me so that I wouldn't bother them. It was bothersome when they felt that my good graces gave them bountiful crops and healthy children and my displeasure was the reason for their horse dying."

"You didn't like their adoration?" I asked.

"I wanted their fear and respect, not their problems," she spat at me. "You things are so weak that you need to always have something to thank or blame for things that are simply nature."

"Fairies are nihilists, then?" I asked. Grenadine stopped pacing and stared at me. I broke out into a cold sweat under that black-eyed stare, thinking that her chatty mood was about to turn abusive again.

"No," she said. There was an undertone of belligerence to that word, but she was still talking, so I assumed that I was still safe.

"We worshipped higher powers and I assume those higher powers worshipped the even higher. Things just get bigger and more unimaginable the deeper you look. To know that you are but a speck on a map of monoliths, well that is humbling even to a fairy," she said.

I was about to ask something else when she threw herself at me. Her small frame was on my lap, black eyes boring holes into me. She reached up and grabbed my left ear and yanked down, like a granny with an unruly child. I yipped at the pain and tried to hold very still, staring back at the fairy, not being defiant, but attempting to show a backbone.

"Why is it that you avoid your mother, Christina?" Grenadine asked, her usually deep voice going high-pitched in a mocking way. "You haven't even told her how close to home you are. I bet she keeps a stash of your little cakes on hand just for you, hoping that you'll surprise her and drop in someday. She just sits on her old, ratty couch and smokes and drinks beer and watches bad television and talks to her friends on the phone about what a great writer you are and what a shit your father was for dying on her. It would be good for her to get a visit from her only child, but here you are avoiding her. You want to have a conversation with me? Then I get to ask the questions, human."

I looked back at her, relishing the feeling of her letting go of my ear. She huffed into my face in disgust and got off of me and flopped back onto my bed, lying on her back and staring at the ceiling like a moody teenager.

"You would think that it was terribly unfair if a family member avoided you like you avoid your mom. How is that okay?" Grenadine said, examining her fingernails.

"She wanted me to stay here and take care of her," I said. "She wanted me to live in that dead-end town and work my ass off so that she could spend my money on Misty's and Coors. She wanted to be my burden."

"It was her turn," Grenadine said. "She worked demeaning jobs to make sure that you always had your little cakes. She gave up on the idea of another man in her life because she knew that you would never be okay with another man taking your father's place, a man who died because he was an alcoholic behind the wheel of a truck that weighed several tons, by the way. He killed a man and his little boy who were going out to get ice cream. He wasn't that great."

"He was a good man with a bad problem," I said, tears welling up in my eyes at the memory of that awful night.

"He certainly wasn't irreplaceable," Grenadine said.

"I loved him," I said.

"So did your mother," Grenadine said, sitting up and giving me a level look.

I furiously wiped at my eyes, angry at the conversation that I was being forced into. Grenadine laughed.

My dad was a trucker. My dad was also an alcoholic. One night while hauling something or other a few towns over, he drunkenly veered into a lane of oncoming traffic on a two-lane road and plowed over a car containing a father and his four-year-old son. My father's truck fell on its side. The man and his son were killed, and my father died from injuries a few hours later. My mother and I got the call that night and we rushed to the hospital. My mom wouldn't let me into the hospital room to see my dad, something I never forgave her for since he later died. But the family of the man and his son came and prayed with my mom in that hospital. They held me on their laps, crying and praying. It was the scariest night of my life up to that point. They were at my father's funeral, assuring my mom that if she ever needed anything, they would help. I've never since known people with such generous and kind dispositions. My mother felt too ashamed to ever contact them again and they faded into memory for me. It was an awful experience, not only because I lost my father, but because I really learned shame.

"Not so fun, is it?" she asked me. "Questions are easier to ask than answer, human."

"My life is working just fine the way it's going right now. My mom understands that I'm very busy. And I am. I'm busy here. I'm not sitting here slouching, I'm working and producing results," I said, a bit of defiance coming out of me. Maybe I wasn't the best daughter in the world, but I wasn't very keen on a murderous fairy calling me out on it.

"You really are wonderful," Grenadine purred. "You are not at all self-aware, my Christina. You really have no idea what a horrible person you are. You are capable of love, you *do* love, but you are so very selective about it. Unless someone earns one of the very few slots in that heart of yours, they are nothing to you. You even have to fake your empathy. It's marvelous to watch you."

I frowned at her, offended by what she said.

"I'm not a horrible person!" I said. "And I don't fake my empathy! I'm polite and I'm warm and I do feel for those people."

"You're polite and you're warm because you know it will make people more at ease with talking to you," Grenadine countered. "And you can stop lying about feeling empathy,

Christina. You know you fake it. You even take the time to wonder why it is that you can't truly feel for the victims you interview."

"If I'm so evil, why am I alive and other evil people end up in that stew pot of yours? Huh? You can't tell me that a seventy-five-cent snack cake has redeemed my evil ways. How am I, the evil manipulator, alive, and Stephanie, who was really guilty only of being ambitious, bits of stew?"

Having her read my brain like it was a bestseller was a huge pain in the ass.

"Your mind really is marvelous," Grenadine said, tilting her head back and looking as if she were hearing her favorite music. "It's art, what I'm doing to you, and your nightmares are my brushstrokes."

"You're playing with me?" I asked, anger and fear boiling together in my chest.

"I'm going to make things very clear for you soon, Christina," Grenadine sneered at me. "But for now, you've got company."

A soft knock at my door nearly scared the greasy contents of my stomach right out of me. I turned to look back at Grenadine and she was gone. That disappearing trick was a devious way to make sure that she always had the last word.

I double checked my appearance in the bathroom mirror and aside from looking abnormally pale and tired, all was well. I looked through the peephole and mouthed a curse at the doorknob before opening it.

"I know you said that you were busy tonight, but something has happened, and I thought that, professionally, you would want to know about it," Terry said to me, brushing past me and into my room.

Of course, I knew what he thought was breaking news. In fact, I knew a hell of a lot more than he did. I had to feign concern and interest.

"Stephanie's car was found abandoned out near that little pond where Matthew Hart's truck was found," Terry said, sinking into an armchair by the window, looking weary.

"Oh no," I said, putting my hands to my face and pushing the picture of Stephanie's head swinging from a hook by its hair out of my head.

"We're trying not to come to any conclusions just yet," he said. "She showed up for work this morning and checked in with some people, but then she said that she had to talk with someone and she wasn't seen or heard from again," he said, putting a large hand over his eyes and looking ready for a nap. I felt a moment of pity for Terry, seeing how he had spent such a large chunk of his day worried about this woman. Whatever their relationship, she meant something to him.

"Terry," I said in my most empathetic voice that I used on the bereaved that I interviewed for the site. "I'm sure maybe she just needed a day of quiet to herself. Maybe it's something else, like she parked her car and went to go sit by the pretty little pond and then decided to go for a walk in the woods and got lost. Has anyone thought to do a search through the woods?"

"No," Terry said. "And there's no reason to. She wore expensive shoes, and she hated bugs and the outdoors. It would be totally out of character for her to go on a spontaneous hike through the woods."

I sat on my bed, looking at him, trying to think of something to say, then ultimately deciding that the less I said, the better. Either Grenadine was pulling more strings than she let on, or the officials in that town were just willfully incompetent. How were they not staking out that pond, seeing as it was obviously the prowling ground for the murderer? And not searching the woods surrounding the pond was beyond careless. I knew that they wouldn't find anything, but they didn't.

"Did she try to contact you at all?" He asked me suddenly. My blood was thundering through my veins with such force that I could actually hear it rushing through my ears. I hoped that my skin tone didn't change and that I was as cool and innocent looking as I was trying to look.

"No," I said. "The most I heard of her wanting to talk to me was what you told me."

Terry sighed and leaned his head back. My eyes caught on his lovely throat for a moment, but I kept my ass planted on the bed and away from him.

"I don't want to be a worry wart," he said. "I don't want to be like my mom and immediately start assuming the worst, but this is so unlike her. In all the years I have known her, she's never gone out of communication before. Never. Not even as a teenager. You could always reach her."

"Maybe she met someone," I said, trying to sound helpful while knowing I was full of shit. "You know, maybe she had a rendezvous going on and they met at the pond and left in his car and she just hasn't gotten back yet. Everybody slips up from their routines sometimes. Everybody."

"You're so sweet to try to make this better on me, honey," he said, looking at me and smiling. "I hope you're right, even though I don't think you are." He got up and sat next to me on the bed, putting a hand comfortably on my upper thigh.

I didn't pull away from him right away, I didn't want to make myself look suddenly frigid towards him because it might draw unwanted attention and suspicion. I let his hand sit there, fingers just inches away from the part of me that he knew too well, smiling into his face as warmly as I could manage. When I felt that I had let a companionable silence sit long enough, I got up from the bed and walked over to the chair at the desk.

"Look, I'm here for you if you need me," I lied. "I really am very busy, please don't think that I'm blowing you off. Feel free to stay here with me or turn the channel on the TV and watch what you want. I just need to get some notes straight and get some writing done."

I hoped that his polite nature would overrule any desire to impose on a busy person and send him away from me. I sat turned in my chair towards him, smiling patiently at him. I saw the hesitation in his face and felt my smile start to become strained.

"No, that's okay, honey," he said, getting up from the bed and making me the most relieved person on the planet. "I've got some stuff of my own to do. Will I see you tomorrow?"

"Sure," I lied.

He leaned down and kissed my forehead, then my cheek, then a wet peck on my lips that I accepted but didn't return. I smiled up at him when he pulled away and he stroked my cheek before he turned and walked to the door.

"I'll talk to you tomorrow, then," he said.

"Okay. Look, I'm sure everything's fine. I'm sure she'll turn up and she'll be horrified at how much worry she's caused," I said, making sure that I looked appropriately concerned.

He smiled at me and blew me a kiss before walking out of the door, closing it quietly behind him. I deflated and slumped back into my chair when he was gone. If that fairy hadn't made sure that I was a witness to what had happened to Stephanie, I could tell Terry to leave me alone with no worries.

CHAPTER THIRTEEN

The next day, a frantic call was put in to the local 911 call center by a woman named Mildred Fleming. According to the call, a box was found on the front desk of the ASPCA where Mrs. Fleming volunteered that contained two severed human hands. Although the police released no name as to whom the hands could have belonged to, Terry told me that it was strongly believed that they belonged to Stephanie D'Agostino because of the manicure and a ring one hand still wore.

I did my best to assure Terry that severed hands didn't mean that she was murdered, that a person could live after having their hands (neatly) removed, but he knew that she had met a gruesome end in a manner very similar to how Matthew Hart and Martin Hamrick had. Terry appeared agonized over this knowledge, but I thought that he was getting off pretty easy considering he didn't see and smell what had truly become of Stephanie in that god-forsaken stew pot. He didn't see the look of fear and helplessness that Stephanie wore right before a gutting knife was plunged into her stomach. He didn't have her glare at him in betrayal as he slunk away from her, leaving her to the fate of the fairy.

I couldn't report more than what was known to the police at the time, and I did my best to keep from writing something that would hurt the investigation, like publishing the theory that the hands belonged to Stephanie before the police made that public knowledge. I still had hopes that the state police detective who had blown me off earlier would eventually talk to me and pissing him off by publishing conjecture was not going to help me. I could confide in my roommate those theories though.

Anais was in a froth over the new turn things had taken. I think that she was telling herself that I was safe from the murderer of this town because so far all of the victims had been men. Once a woman was found to have received that treatment, I was no longer at the bottom of the possible future victims list in Ana's mind.

Her telling me that maybe I should come home meant a lot. The incredible amount of traffic being driven to the site because of that case was more than paying my hotel bill. Anais had even told me that our local newspaper had published a letter to the editor where a reader basically stated that the journalist who profiled Anais, myself, and our site was a prejudiced pig who obviously had never actually visited the site and seen the impressive writing and investigation put into every file. I knew that that had made Anais feel immeasurably better and I felt a twang of pride myself. We both worked very hard and it was wonderful that it was being noticed as such rather than the attention grab that the journalist had tried to make it out to be. But the fact that my ambitious partner was starting to wonder if it was worth it for me to stay in town amused me because I think it was then that I realized that all along I had been every bit as ambitious as Anais. Maybe more.

I did my best to assure Anais that I was going to be just fine. She let the subject of my coming home drop but made sure that I knew that it wasn't closed. I smiled into the phone, hearing the conviction in her voice and relishing her feelings of love and protection towards me.

I hadn't seen Grenadine in over a week. Instead of relaxing, her absence was making me even more paranoid than when she was visiting me daily. If she stayed gone too long, I feared that her crumbling sanity would cause her to forget that we had a sort of rough truce between us. Maybe she would pop into my room with no knowledge of the agreement that she insisted on, and she would instead add me to her stew pot. I'd been dreaming about that stew pot every night since I laid eyes on it. I saw Stephanie's head bobbing in the hot liquid, looking at me in anger. I dreamed that I could smell the stew and that it made my stomach spasm in disturbingly hungry desire as it had when I was there. I dreamed that Grenadine pointed that hooked gutting knife at me and laughed. I slept heavily still, but it stopped being anything resembling peaceful.

I'd relented where Terry was concerned. He wouldn't leave me alone no matter how evasive I tried to be, so I caved and let him take me to dinner and bed a few times. He was still a bit of a vanilla lover, but it was nice having a warm body next to me in bed when I fell asleep. He was in mourning and it was obvious that I was his source of comfort on those nights. I didn't feel good about it, I admit. I wasn't a good person for pretending like I knew nothing about Stephanie's disappearance and I was protecting myself and no one else by manufacturing my ignorance. Still, it was better than uttering the truth of the situation to another person.

The readers of *Killer Chronicles* voted to call the killer that I was supposedly tracking the Appalachian Butcher. My neurotic mind hated the name. I didn't like not being right and I didn't like having to admit that a bunch of internet commenters were better at naming a murderer than I was. I was supposed to be good at stuff like that and that particular failing had played out far too publicly for my liking.

It was a week after Stephanie's "disappearance" that the state police publicly acknowledged that they believed that the hands found at the ASPCA belonged to her. Once this was released, I went through the phone call flaming hoops again to try to get one of the detectives on the case to talk to me. Finally, a Sgt. Todd Blaniar took my call. He was tired, and he didn't want to be talking to me, but he answered my few generic questions amiably enough and gave his permission to use it as an official statement from the state police. It was good for the site to be able to write official statements given directly to me. It helped cement our credibility as investigative journalists rather than sensationalist tabloid writers seeking to exploit people in order to glorify murderers. I guess once a member of the press became one of the victims the police decided to try to be a bit more accommodating when it came to answering questions, and I can't imagine how many phone calls that man had to field on top of his workload, but I was really very appreciative of his time. I made sure to tell him so.

"That's no problem, Ms. Cunningham," he said to me. "You just remember to use this information with respect to the people left behind in the mess that their loved ones' deaths caused."

"We try for that in every case that we cover, sir," I said. "We aren't trying to cause more pain than has already been inflicted."

"That's good," Sgt. Blaniar said before hanging up the phone.

Later that night, I told Terry that I had gotten Sgt. Blaniar to answer some questions and he stopped chewing his hot dog and stared at me with wide eyes.

"What?" I asked.

"Todd Blaniar?" he asked.

"Yeah," I answered.

"That man is really hard-nosed about talking to the media. He would get furious with Stephanie for getting information that he didn't want her to have. The media have rights to get information, but Sgt. Blaniar made it very clear to all of us that he preferred that we be mum about some of the bigger crimes that go on around here. Theft, murder, fatal car accidents, stuff like that. One time, there was this car accident on I-79 and Stephanie got the name of the victim before the police released it and she posted it on the paper's Facebook page, where the victim's family saw it and the police caught heck from the family for taking so long to inform them. Blaniar was furious," Terry said, resuming his hot dog consumption. I smiled at his use of the word "heck" instead of "hell." Terry had a hell of a long stick up his ass.

"Was it you who told Stephanie the name?" I asked, still smiling.

"Course it was me," he said. "I shouldn't have told her the name so soon, I knew better than to trust her to use discretion, but I ain't always wearing my smartest head. I was more careful with what I told her after that. Like I said, the public has the right to know certain things, but those things need to be handled in a way that she didn't seem to fully grasp."

He placed the half-eaten hot dog down into the wax paper-clad basket and stared at the table pensively. I looked at him for a minute, waiting for him to speak again. When he didn't, I threw a French fry at him. He looked up and gave me one of his devastatingly gorgeous smiles. The man could have been on the cover of *GQ*.

"I shouldn't speak ill of the dead," he said, the smile melting from his features. "She was my friend. I'm being unfair."

"Everybody has a bad side, Terry," I said. "You got to see it more than most because of your close relationship. But you saw her good side too, and you must have seen it more than the bad side if you two stayed close for so long, right?"

"Eh," he shrugged.

"There's no shame in truly knowing someone, bad side and all," I said.

"Well, we weren't always just friends," he said softly, watching his large hands pick at his hot dog bun. I was about to snatch the thing out of its basket and finish it myself. West Virginia really has the best hot dogs and T&L were a favorite of mine since childhood. I'd eat four or five in one sitting, no problem. I was also hyper-focused on the hot dog because I *really* didn't want to listen to him confess to having had sex with Stephanie a few dozen times over the years.

"I'm thinking about getting another dog," I said.

"Wait, let me say this," he said. I sighed loudly and settled back into my chair.

"Stephanie and I weren't always purely platonic friends," he said. "On more than one occasion, we made love."

I tried not to cringe. I find the term "making love" to be a phrase used by people who are too intimidated by the word "sex." For such a fun activity, it should be more commonly referred to by some of the more playful terms. Boinking, screwing, fucking, banging, boning, nailing, or having sex. "Making love" just added connotations to the act that made me feel icky, and I certainly didn't feel any real love towards Terry, who I had just 'sproinged' before offering to treat him to hot dogs.

"Terry, I don't need to know this," I said firmly.

"I want you to know," he said, reaching out and taking my hand. "I am finding myself maybe almost in love with you."

That "aw shucks" thing would have worked on me like a tonic at any other time, but it upset me then and there. Terry professing feelings for me was a cluster fuck that I really did not need in my life.

"I've made a big mistake," I said to him.

"What?" He asked, taken aback by my reaction to his romantic words.

"Terry, I do not have a place in my life for love or anything serious. Now, I came into this with the understanding that this was casual. I live six hours away. I travel a lot and I've got some personal things going on that make having a serious, loving relationship with you flat-out impossible," I said, trying to remain calm.

"But," he stammered. "You've been there for me during this rough time. You've comforted me and made love to me in my time of pain. You've been a compassionate and soulful person to me during this whole affair. Christina, how can you say that you don't feel the same for me?"

"Because I don't," I said. "Terry, I don't want to hurt you, but this was always supposed to be temporary. I mean, *you* set the terms."

"Well I can't help how I feel," he said, crossing his arms over his chest and pouting. He was actually pouting.

"Neither can I," I countered, getting up and walking out of the restaurant. We had come together in my car, but I figured he could get a ride back to the hotel to get his truck easily enough, so I didn't feel bad about leaving him in there by himself.

Nearly an hour later, I was sitting in my hotel room stewing on the situation at the restaurant for two reasons. One, I was very unhappy that my fuck buddy was trying to put the emotional moves on me. Two, I really did want another hot dog and had left before I got the opportunity to do so.

I was pacing the room, seriously considering going back for a takeout box of hot dogs when a harsh knock at my door scared the hell out of me. I walked to the door and looked out of the peephole to see that it was an agitated Terry. I put my forehead onto the door, closed my eyes, and fully prepared myself to not answer the door. He knocked again, more softly this time.

"Please let me in," he said.

"Please stop this," I said.

"Christina," he began. "Please. I have more to say. I told you that I love you, not that I want to get married and make you give up your way of life for me. Surely there's some way for us to make this work."

"Terry, there's nothing to make work. This was a casual fling and nothing more. I do not return your feelings," I said. We were talking softly to each other through the door, and I preferred that to having him in my room, trying to touch me as he talked. Having a door between us was safer.

"I don't believe you," he said. "I think you're just saying that to keep a distance between us so that it won't be hard on you when you have to leave here. But Christina, it doesn't have to be this way. I've got no problem changing up my schedule so that I'm off on Fridays, and I can drive to you on Friday and spend the weekends with you. Over time, who knows? You were originally a local girl, you've got roots around here. And you can do your job remotely. This has a lot of possibilities to it."

"Leaving here is not going to cause me even the slightest bit of pain, Terry, I promise. Also? I work online. I understand the reach of the internet. If I wanted to keep something going with you, I do understand how totally doable that is thanks to technology," I said.

"Who hurt you?" he asked me suddenly.

In the movies, this is the scene where the hard woman's frozen heart melts and she opens the door, her eyes welling with tears of true love and she leaps into the arms of the man who is there to save her from her hurtful past. Thank fucking God that I don't live in a movie because my reaction was so much better than that.

I punched the door. That hurt, and I doubled over keeping myself quiet. I didn't want Terry to hear my groaning and squealing because my stupid self punched a really hard door. Then I kicked the door. I looked out through the peephole and saw Terry looking startled. I kicked the door again and smiled when I saw him jump.

"Go away Terry," I said softly. "We're done here. Thanks for your help."

I stayed at the peephole and watched him stare at the door for a minute, then look down the hallway before finally stepping away from the door and walking away. I breathed out a long sigh of relief and slumped against the door. With that tie severed, I was one step closer to finishing up and going home.

Flowers were sent to my room the next day. They were pretty peach lilies in a glass vase. The card read, "Please feel free to call or text. Yours always, Terry. XOXO"

I threw them in the dumpster behind the hotel.

My tensions were getting to an all-time high even as Anais assured me that my updates were pulling in millions upon millions of views. Grenadine's absence had me extremely worried. I still wasn't sure if I could leave town without her knowing and I was concerned that I was going to have to stay in that damned Holiday Inn until Anais dragged me out. I really wished for it all to be over. I wanted her to give me that stupid gift or whatever so that I could go home and start enjoying the fruits of my labor.

CHAPTER FOURTEEN

T hings were slowing down on the investigation. Every lead the police checked out took them to a dead end. I interviewed Mildred Fleming, the lady who discovered Stephanie's hands in a box and got close to nothing from her. She was an older lady and all she could say in regards to Stephanie was "bless her heart," which is not exactly quotable. Anais had brought up my coming home again and I knew that I wouldn't be able to put her off much longer. Things either needed to start picking up or I was going to have to chance mine and Anais' safety by going home.

I was sitting at the bar of the steak house next to my hotel drinking a beer and eating jalapeño poppers when Terry sat down next to me. I lowered my beer and gave him a sidelong glance before I resumed my brooding. I was trying to enjoy my first truly satisfying meal of junk in days. I'd been eating salads and brown rice and grilled chicken, and I was sick to death of not having the awesome slickness of grease on my lips. I wasn't happy about having my self-destructive eating disturbed by the twerp.

"You haven't been answering my texts," he said quietly.

"That's because I blocked you," I replied.

"Why would you do that?" he asked, taken back.

"Because I told you to leave me alone and you're not listening," I said.

"Look, I need to talk to you about other stuff," he said, his voice low and conspiratorial.

"Okay, get on with it so I can enjoy my junk food in peace, please," I said.

"As a matter of procedure, I was questioned about Stephanie's disappearance. You know, like the last time I talked to her and all that. It appears that I was the last person that she texted, and I had to name you as my alibi.

I'm really sorry, but I had to be honest. I work with those people," he blurted.

I looked over at him, frowning in surprise at his outburst.

"Look, I said I was sorry," he said. "If it helps, I let them know that we have feelings for each other and that you are *not* a loose woman."

I burst out laughing.

"Now don't start being cruel again, honey," Terry said to me.

"I'm not being cruel," I said, wiping tears from my eyes. "I understand that I'm your alibi and I'll back you up, no problem. I have no issue with any of these people knowing that we've been having sex, Terry. I mean really, in this day and age it should not be so shocking to people that consenting adults carry on perfectly lovely casual sexual relationships while also being morally upstanding citizens. Stop with that puritanical stuff, for Pete's sake."

"I wasn't being puritanical," he said sourly. "I was just making sure that you knew that I had your reputation and best interests in the front of my mind."

"Yeah, well you can go ahead and let those worries sink to the back, Terry, because I'm a big girl and I've got nothing to be ashamed of," I said.

"Won't you unblock me, Christina? Won't you stop being stubborn and think about my offer, honey?" he said, leaning closer to me. I leaned away from him and slammed my bottle of Yuengling on the bar.

"You can stop with the pet names. You can just stop altogether, damn it," I said in a low quiet voice. "My answer was given to you in a very clear and concise way and I've said all I want to say on the matter. Now go away, Terry, before I make a big scene making it look like you're doing something untoward. You're local. They know you and you'd forever be labeled a woman-harassing creep."

Terry huffed at me and loudly got up from the bar and left me on my own. I smiled at the bartender, who was an older fellow that night, and continued my contemplative noshing.

About an hour later, I was walking back to the hotel. It was dark out, but there were a lot of lights keeping everything from being too creepy. I'd done this walk in the dark a few times and felt mostly secure. I still tried to stay aware of my surroundings and any people out and about, but mostly this was a mundane stroll through a parking lot.

"I think I'm getting an idea," a voice said beside me.

I squealed and jumped, grabbing my chest to keep my heart from making a hasty retreat to one of the cars parked nearby. Grenadine was walking next to me companionably. I heard her before I saw her. She was walking around as Nummy Nellie again.

"Long time no see," I muttered, resuming my walk and taking a calming breath. My evening just kept getting shittier and shittier.

"That wet blanket is complicating your life," Grenadine said to me, looking straight ahead as we walked. "I knew that I was going to have to do something about him."

"No!" I said, turning quickly and holding my hands out in a *stop* motion. "Please don't. He's a mild problem at most and I think I've driven my point home to him. Please don't do anything to that man. He's a good person and he's too handsome to go into that stew pot."

"If you call *that* handsome," she said, sneering.

"I do, actually. He's pretty much perfect looking," I said.

"And look what good it has gotten you," she said.

"He's not a bad man," I said. "He's annoying and he's a bit of a gossip, but none of that paints him as bad. He doesn't deserve to die."

"I get to decide what he deserves. You're not a good person, Christina. As much as you try to make people think you are, you are not an empathetic or concerned person at all. You care about a select few and the rest of the world can go straight to hell as far as you're concerned. Look how cold you're being to this idiot, Terry. He sincerely cares about you, and your reaction to that is to push him away from you so that you don't have to be tied down by another man's waning libido. Admit it, that's what it is. They stay lively in the beginning, but then football season starts, beer guts start to pop out, and they start to go down to once a week, once a month, and then you find yourself locked in the bathroom watching porn on your phone and taking care of yourself in secret so that his fragile ego doesn't take a hit. Isn't that right?"

"You're picking out the worst of my thoughts," I argued. I was in an arguing mood with the fairy and I should have known better. Was it her long absence? Was it her threat to Terry? It wasn't smart, no matter the reason.

"I think things like that in my worst moments. Everybody has those, damn it. But I try to keep my chin up, especially where other people are concerned. I don't really think those horrible things about all men. Isaac was one guy. I know that, I get it. I don't want to be one of those people who have one bad experience and blame an entire demographic. Not all men are like Isaac. Not all men are cheating pigs. Not all men are sweet but bland like Terry. And I'm not a bad person walking around in a nice person disguise either! Maybe I disconnect myself a little too much sometimes, but for my own sanity, I don't want to think too hard about what I'm writing about," I said.

"Thou doth protest too much, Christina," Grenadine said. "Deep down you know you're not the nicest person. You do. I can see it in that head of yours. You know it."

I chewed on the inside of my cheek, thinking. I was walking to the elevators in the hotel trailed by Nummy Nellie from hell, trying to look into my own soul to see if it was as dirty as the fairy was trying to say. I couldn't see how caring for only a few people in my life made me bad. There simply wasn't enough of me to care for every damned person I encountered. And the people I did care for? I'd die or kill for them.

"You'd kill for them, maybe. But I don't think you'd die for them," Grenadine said, listening in on my racing thoughts.

"Fear of death makes me bad?" I asked.

"There's no nobility to you. I like you, but you're a weak thing," Grenadine answered.

"What does that even mean?" I said, punching the "3" in the elevator.

"Never mind, Christina," Grenadine said patiently.

"Grenadine," I said, using her name for the first time in conversation with her. She looked at me seriously.

"Please. Please don't hurt Terry," I pleaded.

"You care for him more than you let on?" she asked, mocking me.

"You know the answer to that," I said, unlocking my room and letting her in before me.

"Yes, I do. So why all the fuss? How can you be bothered about his fate one way or another?" she asked.

"Because I don't want to think about another person going into the awful pot of yours!" I yelled. "I'm going to have nightmares for the rest of my life about that fucking pot and what you did to Stephanie. And why Stephanie? I've done the research and Martin Hamrick and Matthew Hart were sort of horrible people. It's not that I condone it, but they were bad. Why did Stephanie deserve that? Being manipulative and ambitious are not worthy of a death sentence."

"You don't get to question my motives, human," Grenadine replied tartly. "And I'm being very indulgent with you in letting you give me your opinion on my favor to you. That's what it would be, Christina. Getting Terry out of your hair would be me gracing you with good fortune. You don't like him, he won't go away on his own, so I'd make him."

"That is not at all helpful to me in the long run," I said, sinking into the arm chair by the bed. Grenadine paced nearby.

"Your long run should be my concern?" she asked, cocking an eyebrow at me.

"I didn't say that! You're the one so concerned with making sure this favor is perfect. Killing the guy I've been sleeping with isn't going to help me. It's going to complicate my life with having to answer questions and the most I would get is a small piece on the site where I could lament having known and worked with him. There's no real help there. The real help that I need is being able to finish my work here and going home and I have no idea how that's supposed to happen. Unless the police are huge dunderheads and pin these murders on some poor guy and arrest him and I can make it out like the killer has been arrested, this file will be open forever and listed as a mystery and that's just not good for us," I said, ranting.

I was just letting off steam. I was tired and I was cranky and I wanted more than anything to be done with the fairy and to go home to Anais. If I'd known that Grenadine was seriously listening to my words and not just dismissing me as a grump, I would have kept my damned mouth shut. Her eyes were twinkling, and a wide smile was breaking the sweetness of her Nummy Nellie face. I felt my skin go clammy at the sight and goose bumps prickled my entire body.

"Bingo," she said, and I knew that I had fucked up in a very major way with my big fat mouth.

In an instant, I was no longer sitting in the semi-comfortable armchair in my hotel room, but rather I was sitting on a carpeted floor in someone's living room. I was facing a small, flat screen television and I heard a man's voice squawk in surprise behind me. I recognized the squawk. I closed my eyes and buried my face in my hands. This was not good. So not good.

I turned and saw Terry, who had been sitting in a big cozy looking recliner in his underwear before we popped in on him. Now he was crouched on the seat of the chair, looking at us with wide, panicked eyes. I couldn't blame him. Grenadine's popping in and out act scared the shit out of me too.

Grenadine wasn't playing. Her adorable Nummy Nellie skin was gone, and Terry got an eyeful of the fairy in her true, oddly colored glory. He opened a drawer in the small table next to his chair and pulled out a handgun and pointed it at Grenadine. His eyes looked to me in panic. I'm certain that I looked as scared as I felt. I felt my chest heaving with my own panicked breathing as I watched Grenadine staring Terry down, advancing on him slowly.

"Christina," Terry said to me, keeping his gun pointed steadily at Grenadine. "Honey, what is going on?"

"You just be silent now, little dog," Grenadine said.

"Stay back," Terry said. I marveled at how level he was being considering that it was obvious that we had startled him almost to the point of soggy shorts.

"And what exactly are you going to do if I don't?" Grenadine asked. "Hmm?"

"I said stay back!" Terry screamed.

Grenadine kept advancing and Terry pulled the trigger, making me jump and cover my ears. Nothing happened. Grenadine wasn't affected. Nothing behind her exploded into splinters or shards. There was a deafening bang, and then nothing. Terry looked at his gun in confusion and then fired another shot at the still-advancing fairy. Again, nothing.

He raised the gun to fire again, but Grenadine sped to him and knocked him into a sitting position on the chair, her crouching on his lap. He screamed as she lifted the hand holding the gun to her mouth and she neatly bit off his index finger. The gun fell away, and she pulled the finger from her mouth and examined it. Terry held his bleeding hand, panting heavily and staring into Grenadine's black-eyed face.

"Give me that hand, little dog," Grenadine soothed. "I need you unscathed so that you can be a proper favor to my sweet Christina."

"Guns are so indelicate," Grenadine continued. "I'd have respected you more had you come at me with a spoon. A gun is a baby blanket for insecure little boys who like to parade around as men. *A man* would know better."

Guns are indelicate huh? I thought. *And biting someone's finger off isn't?*

"Be quiet!" Grenadine screamed at me. "Just keep your spineless opinions to yourself!"

Terry's eyes shot to me, a look of horror on his face. I hadn't said anything out loud and to him, Grenadine looked more unhinged than she actually was. I could see that he was about to speak, but before he could, Grenadine smashed his bitten finger back onto the stub on his hand and he screamed out in pain.

"Hush," Grenadine soothed. "Healing is painful, human."

Terry gritted his teeth and made pained noises for a few more seconds before Grenadine released his hand. He held it up in amazement, wiggling his index finger.

"What in God's name..." he began.

"Look at me, dog," Grenadine soothed.

I was still sitting on the floor watching this from about ten feet away. My point of view was of Grenadine's back and Terry's pale stricken face. When his eyes locked on Grenadine's, I watched them lose all of their luster and shine, which was really very dramatic because his eyes had teared up a lot when his finger was bitten off. It was like watching a time-lapse video of a pond draining and drying out.

Terry convulsed, his back arching into Grenadine and he made a choking sound. Grenadine's hand shot out and landed on his broad, bare chest. His eyes were still locked on hers, bulging and dimming at the same time. His face was turning purple. I got up from my seated position, keeping my distance but feeling panicked that Grenadine was killing him.

"Stop it!" I screamed. "Stop hurting him!"

Grenadine turned her head slightly so that I could see her face in profile. She was smiling.

Terry continued to struggle against her small hand on his chest for a moment more before he relaxed back into his cushy looking chair, panting. Grenadine reached out and lightly brushed a piece of hair off of his forehead. He didn't seem to notice. His eyes were closed, and he had started sweating. Grenadine nimbly hopped off of his lap and took a seat on his equally cushy sofa, watching him intently. When he started whimpering, I went to him.

I knelt by his chair and reached out, touching his face. He was extremely hot, alarmingly so.

"What did you do to him?" I asked Grenadine. "He's fevered. His brain will cook if he stays this hot!"

"Be quiet," Grenadine said. "He's not going to die. I'm not going to kill him."

I looked over at her, startled. Confused. Relieved.

"I am sorry, though," she continued. "For what's about to happen to you."

CHAPTER FIFTEEN

I was about to ask Grenadine what in the hell she was talking about when Terry's hand shot out from his lap and grabbed a handful of my hair, yanking to the side so that my head wrenched down, my neck popping in a scary way.

"No pain no gain," Grenadine said behind me. "Isn't that the saying? It's true. Just suffer through this, little human, and you'll have what you want from me."

Terry got up from his recliner, jerking me up to my own feet in the process. I struggled, trying to pry his hands open and striking out at his body, trying to land a hit even though I couldn't see anything from the way my head was angled. I was being dragged down a narrow hallway, fighting the whole way.

"Terry, let me go! What are you doing? Stop this! Stop! Let me go!" I was saying over and over again. He did not listen. He kept dragging me away by my hair. I heard a door open and was dragged through a doorway and then thrown by my hair onto a bed.

I landed face-first and spun around to look at Terry and get away, but he was on top of me before I could begin to scurry. He punched me in the jaw, sending me back onto the bed, seeing black and red spots blur my vision. I stayed back and stunned until he started ripping at my clothes, trying to strip me.

Something in my brain, something primal and made of fear, started beating on the inside of my skull. I closed my eyes as tightly as I could and started screaming as loud as I could, shredding my throat. I struck out and landed as many hits as I could, but he would not stop tearing at my clothes, cutting the soft skin of my body as seams shredded and sunk in. I hit him in the face, I scratched and slapped and tried to dig my thumbs into his eyes. He shrugged off my attempts at self-defense. He was so much bigger and stronger than me. His heavy weight on my legs kept me from being able to kick.

He hit my jaw again, making me black out for a few seconds. When I came to, my pants were off, my breasts were exposed, and he was standing over me, sliding his boxer briefs down his hips. I was groggy, and my head felt like someone had dropped an anvil on it, but I started scooting away from him in a panic. He reached out easily and grabbed my ankle, dragging me back towards him. I fought him by clenching my legs together, but it didn't last long. He wrenched them open and placed his body between them in an infuriatingly easy way.

I was screaming and pleading with him, trying to scoot away from him but he just pinned me down and barreled into me. I screamed in pain, feeling myself tear and bruise from the inside. I continued to fight, but then the biting started.

As he pounded me relentlessly, he held onto my neck with one hand, a thumb over the front of my throat as if reminding me that a simple squeeze was all that he needed to shut me up. He lowered his head down to my shoulder and bit. He bit hard. I screamed louder and harder, but I could feel my voice giving. Blood was starting to make the back of my throat get gooey and clogged. I was coughing when he bit my breast. I was screaming when he bit my neck.

The police were beating on the door when I was able to comprehend anything other than the pain. Terry got off of me and I noticed that he had my blood all over his face, like he had rubbed his face in it, and there was blood on his softening penis. I rolled onto my side, curling into a ball, my back to my rapist. I was shaking uncontrollably, and my breath was coming out in harsh, painful wheezes.

"Mister Knight! This is the police! Open the door and come out with your hands above your head!" I heard the police command from outside. We must have been close to the front door but seeing as I popped into the living room via crazy fairy, I couldn't know.

"She's got to be next!" Terry screamed. "She found out and was going to write about it! She has to be next!"

I stayed curled up in a ball, feeling pain in places I'd never felt such agony, my eyes closed and running water freely.

"Come out, now!" the police commanded.

"I have a gun! I'll end it all!" Terry screamed back. "She knew too much! She got too close!"

The sound of Terry's front door crashing inward made me jump, but I kept my eyes closed. I heard Terry slam his bedroom door shut as I heard many feet thumping down the hallway towards us.

"Mister Knight! Open the door and come out with your hands above your head!" the police commanded.

"Terry! Open the goddamn door and surrender! What in the hell are you doing in there, boy?" another voice screamed.

"No!" Terry screamed.

"OPEN THE DOOR! LAST WARNING!" the second voice screamed again.

"She has to die!" Terry screamed.

A moment later, I heard a loud crashing, splintering sound and many thumps and shouts as the police burst into the bedroom and tackled Terry to the floor. I took a moment to slowly open my weary eyes. If I'd had a voice left, I would have squealed at Grenadine's face inches from mine. She was kneeling beside the bed, staring at me, her black eyes regarding me coolly.

"This is a great favor I'm paying you, Christina. I've made it look like that wet rag of yours has been a very, very bad boy and he's going to get blamed for things he didn't do, all so you can get that much-desired acclaim. The word of a survivor is much more savory to the public than the word of a hungry, ambitious reporter." She reached out a hand and stroked my cheek gently.

"Now all you have to do," she whispered to me. "Is ask yourself how much you want it."

Then she was gone. Someone touched my bare shoulder and I jerked away from the hand and fell off of the bed.

"She's alive!" I heard a man shout. "She needs medical attention and a blanket! Get an ambulance out here now!"

Many "yessirs!" followed and someone knelt down beside me and covered me with the comforter off of Terry's bed. I stayed curled up on the floor, not wanting to look at anybody. I couldn't bear being seen and not having to look at the people looking at me let me keep at least that part of me numb while the rest of me was screaming in pain.

"Ma'am? Ma'am, an ambulance is coming. We'll get you taken care of. You're safe now." A hand reached out again and patted my shoulder. I shuddered and jerked away, trying to wheeze a demand that I not be touched.

I felt the man's presence kneeling beside me, not letting me be alone, as some scuffles continued. I heard authoritative stomps coming towards the room a moment before I heard a new voice.

"Is this the victim?" a man asked softly.

"Yes sir," the man kneeling behind me said quietly.

"Got a name?" the bossy voice asked.

There was no vocal response. I assume the man kneeling by me just shook his head.

"Let me know where they take her," the bossy voice said before stomping out.

"JESUS CHRIST, HEY GET OUT HERE!" I heard someone scream from just outside of the window that was above where I was curled up.

"What is it?" I heard the bossy voice ask.

"There's blood everywhere in here, Todd! It's his fucking murder shed!" the first voice said.

I wondered what they were talking about.

I was cold and in so much pain I couldn't think on one subject for very long. I was surrounded by noise and movement, but all I could be at the time was a ball of pain and fear. My jaw hurt. My shoulder and breast and neck felt like they were missing chunks of flesh, but I was too scared to reach up and find out. My thighs and tender intimate places were throbbing and aching in a way that no amount of curling up or wriggling would take away. I wanted Anais. I wanted someone to call Anais.

I turned as best as I could to see the man kneeling by me. He was looking at me, alerted by my movement. He was about my age, early 30s. He reached a hand out to still me, but thankfully stopped short of actually touching me.

"You just stay still now, ma'am," he said to me. "That ambulance will be here very soon."

"Can you call my roommate?" I tried to say. It came out as a harsh whisper and I was reminded of my shredded throat. I tried to hold back the cough that came from my attempt to talk, but it came anyhow, and my entire body lit up with fresh pain and agony with the spasm. When the cough subsided, I was gasping in pain and I could hear the poor cop behind me fidgeting, trying to decide how to help me without touching me.

"I'm sorry, I can't hear what you're saying," he said to me quietly. "You just stay still. I think that ambulance is here. But I'll stay here with you, don't you worry."

I closed my eyes against the wall of tears building up over them and the warm spill of new salty water was almost comforting. It was the only warmth in my life then. I hoped that I would remember the kindness of the man kneeling behind me.

The paramedics came in a clamor of rattles and stomps, asking the cop in the room with me to step away so that they could get to me. A hand fell on my shoulder and I began shaking uncontrollably at the hand, trying to get it off of me.

"Alright, hold on, we need to get her on the stretcher," a soft female voice said.

"Ma'am, if you can move, we need you to stretch out and get on this stretcher for us," a man's voice said.

"She's really traumatized," I heard the cop say.

"Okay, alright," the female voice said. "Eric, help me lift her."

Hands were all over me. I couldn't get them off. They were touching places on me that hurt. They were touching places Terry had pulled and pounded and slammed and bitten. I was crying as they maneuvered my body to lie flat on my back on a cool, hard stretcher. I kept my eyes shut tightly as hands adjusted Terry's comforter around my body to maintain modesty. I was tucked in like a scared child after a nightmare about the thing under the bed. I wished it were that easy. I was living a nightmare about the thing in the pond.

I was given a lovely shot of something in the back of that ambulance that made my body feel warm and heavy, but there was no more pain. The two paramedics, a round pink woman with kind brown eyes and an older scruffy man fussed over me, looking at my face and talking quietly to each other. They asked me my name and I whispered it as best as I could to the kind looking woman. She was writing on one of those scary metal clipboards that always make me think of morgues.

With my mind clouded by that blessed shot, I wasn't quite sure, but it seemed that my ambulance ride was strangely lengthy. Terry must have lived far out in the sticks.

I asked for Anais, hoping that the kind woman was writing that down on her morgue clipboard.

"Please call Ana," I said. "I want her here with me. Call Ana. Ana will know how to make this better. Call Ana."

I was vaguely aware of being awakened by movement. There was darkness above me and then blindingly bright lights. People kept trying to ask me questions, but the shot was so amazing, and I was so relaxed that I couldn't be bothered to really even focus on what exactly was being said to me. I was warm, and it felt safe to be warm after being so cold and in so much pain while waiting to be taken out of Terry's house. I wanted to lie in quiet while enjoying being warm. I wanted everybody to be quiet. I wanted Anais to sit with me and tell me to remember to breathe. I wanted a Zebra Cake to fill my mouth with sweetness and send a wave of comfort and happiness over me. I didn't want to wake up and think about Terry's dead eyes staring into me as he beat and raped me.

CHAPTER SIXTEEN

I was allowed that first night and half of the next day to languish in a drugged-out sleep. When I woke up, Anais was in the room with me, pushing buttons on the television remote in agitation. My movements alerted her to my wakefulness and she came to me and hugged me fiercely, her tears warming the side of my face. I grunted, her beautiful hug causing me quite a lot of pain. I hoped she didn't hear it.

"Girl, I always said that your luck was shit," she said, pulling away and looking at my face. She saw something that made her cringe and she turned away, pulling something out of her oversized bag. It was a box of Sunny Cakes, a Nummy Nellie treat. It was like presenting a glass of water to a person fresh out of a ten-mile hike in the Sahara.

I was so grateful that Anais was there that I burst into tears at the sight of that box of treats. She dropped the box onto the bed beside me and wrapped her arms around me again, holding me tight. This time I ignored the pain. I breathed in the smell of her spicy perfume and relished her warmth as she held me, protecting me.

After we had both calmed down a bit, Anais offered to call my mom. I really didn't want my mom there freaking out over me, but there was no getting around it. She could see all about the mess on the news and it wouldn't be fair for her to hear about her daughter being attacked from a news anchor.

The next bit of business was having the rape kit done. I was humiliated at being taken to a cold examination room without Anais, alone with a doctor and a nurse. They explained every step of the process to me and asked if it was alright if they continue at every turn. If I was uncomfortable with something, it wasn't done. I was thankful for their tact, but I still had to submit to a vaginal swab, a mouth swab, and having stuff scraped from under my fingernails. They combed my pubic area for pubic hairs not belonging to me, photographed me inside and out, and asked a lot of uncomfortable questions. It took nearly three hours and I was grateful when they handed me a slip of paper with the number to my rape kit on it. I was sore all over again and wishing that I could have another one of those shots that reminded me of what it felt like to be warm and safe.

That evening, Sgt. Todd Blaniar himself came to my bedside to talk to me. It hurt to sit up in bed too much. The parts of me that were typically beneath me in a seated position had taken a hell of a beating and lying back was most comfortable physically, but it was uncomfortable talking to a strange man in that position.

"Hello, Sergeant," I croaked when he'd introduced himself in a stiff and formal manner. "We talked on the phone once and you told me to treat everybody with respect, remember?"

"Yes, Ms. Cunningham. I remember you," he answered. He looked like he hadn't slept in a decade and the sweat stains around the collar of his shirt and the stink of stale coffee wafting off of him told me that I was almost correct in that assumption.

I'd had some quiet time that day to think about what had happened. I needed to get out of my own sphere of pain and misery and try to figure out exactly what the hell had gone on the night before. Grenadine had done something to Terry that made him go berserk and do those things to me. I truly did not believe that he would have been capable of doing what he did otherwise.

I was still foggy on a few points, but I had every intention of grilling the poor tired Sgt. Blaniar about it. What was the murder shed? Had Terry talked and confessed to anything? What did I find that he kept screaming about to the police? Had he snapped out of whatever Grenadine had done to him and was he sorry for what he had done to me? I needed to know. I also needed to be careful. I couldn't talk about Grenadine at all, which meant that I was going to be lying through my teeth when giving my statement.

Everybody already knew that Terry and I were having a fling, so hopefully nothing that I said was going to be too far-fetched.

"How are you feeling?" Sgt. Blaniar asked me.

"I'm pretty sore," I answered honestly. "They've taken me off whatever major shots they were pumping into me and putting me on Percocet. My roommate is at the pharmacy now filling the 'scrip.' She had also taken my sobbing mother with her which was a blessing. Anais always knew the best course of action. Always.

He sat down on a chair by my bed and pulled out a pad of paper and a pen from his front shirt pocket.

"I need you to tell me about last night. Start from the beginning and take your time," he said.

I'd practiced this, so I didn't pause or look like I was thinking too much.

"Well, Terry and I had a sort of fling going on while I was in town. It was supposed to be really casual, his idea, and it was nice until he started acting strange," I said.

"Strange how?" Sgt. Blaniar asked.

"He started professing feelings of love for me and he wouldn't leave me alone when I tried to break things off with him," I answered.

"So how did you end up at his house last night?" he asked me.

"I was out to dinner at this steak house next to my hotel. It's the Holiday Inn out there, do you know the one?" I asked. He nodded at me, scribbling in his notebook, so I continued.

"I was sitting at the bar having a beer and some food when he came in and sat next to me. This was uninvited, mind you. He wanted to tell me that he had had to use me as an alibi when questioned about the disappearance of Stephanie D'Agostino and that I needed to go along with it."

"Was the alibi that he gave to the police not true?" he asked me.

"I brought him breakfast at his place of work that morning, but I had an interview with Bridget Maditz at

McDonald's at about mid-morning and I didn't see him again until late that night when he came to my hotel room to tell me about Stephanie's disappearance," I answered honestly. I'd been slightly worried before things went to hell for me that Terry using me as an alibi might have been murky since I had only been with him in the early morning, but he was an honest man and surely he had a reputation as such. That would have been good cushioning in case there were gaps in his story. That, and he actually was innocent of anything happening to Stephanie.

"Alright, so back at the steak house, he tells you to go along and be his alibi, then what?" Sgt. Blaniar probed.

"I told him that I would go along with it," I confessed. "But then I asked him to leave me alone and after a few more words, he left. About an hour later, I was walking back to my room when he drove up to me in his truck and asked me to go for a ride with him. I was tired of him bothering me, but he really did seem like a harmless man. He'd been gentle and kind, albeit a bit annoying and hard to get rid of. I agreed to take the ride so that I could try to convince him that I didn't want to have any sort of real relationship with him and to leave me alone."

"Mmhmm," Sgt. Blaniar probed, still writing.

"He took me to his house and I sat down in his living room thinking he'd offer me a drink and we'd have a serious talk, maybe go to bed together one last time, then he'd take me back to my hotel. But that's not what happened. He started pacing around the room, really agitated and he kept asking me what I knew about him that was making me want to break it off with him. I didn't know what he was talking about, I just kept trying to convince him that I wasn't on the market for anything other than a casual hook-up kind of relationship. I mean, I live six hours away in Reading, Pennsylvania. Seriously, a long-term relationship between two busy people is just stupid wishful thinking. But he kept asking me what I knew, what I had found out. I kept telling him I didn't know, but he kept telling me that I was lying and that I knew too much. That's when he attacked me," I said. I was surprised at how easily the words came out of me.

"Okay," Sgt. Blaniar said, leaning forward so that his elbows were on his thighs. His eyes were wide and full of concern. "I need you to recount that for me. Take your time."

I didn't want to recount that part. At all. I didn't want to have to put into words what had happened to me at the hands of that gentle man. A gentle man who was under the spell of a lunatic fairy with a superiority complex. I dug deep and made myself tell Sgt. Blaniar about the hair pulling, the punches to the jaw, the raping, and the biting. I felt my throat tighten up when I talked about the rape even though I was doing my best to tell it in the coldest, most disconnected way possible. The fear that I felt when he started tearing away my clothes never left me. It sort of pooled in my being and seeped into tiny cracks to hide, always there, always punching me in the gut at the memory of it all.

"Can you tell me who stayed with me while we waited for the ambulance to come?" I asked Sgt. Blaniar when I had told the tale of my attack. He raised his eyebrows in surprise and then appeared to be thinking, trying to recount who it was he saw in there kneeling next to me when he walked into that room.

"I believe that it was Adam Wetzel who stayed with you. Why?" he asked.

"He was very kind to me," I whispered, tears flooding my eyes. "I was going to send him some flowers."

"Well that makes me happy to hear," Sgt. Blaniar said to me, a small smile causing the corners of his eyes to crinkle. "I have one more question for you and then I'll let you get some rest. There was a handgun in Mr. Knight's living room that had been fired three times. Mr. Knight had traces of gunpowder on his hand and wrist and that is consistent with the theory that he had fired the gun recently. Do you know anything about that?"

I sure as hell did.

"No," I lied. "I didn't even see a gun. But I wasn't looking around much, not after he started raving at me."

"Alright," Sgt. Blaniar said, putting his pad and pen away, standing up. "Thank you for your time, Ms. Cunningham. Get well soon."

"Sergeant?" I said. "Could you wait a second?"

He stopped and looked down at me. I propped myself up on my elbows to try to look more dignified.

"My work isn't done yet," I said seriously. "Will it be alright to get the information on all of this so that I can close this file on my website?"

His mouth dropped open and he frowned down at me in disbelief.

"You have to be tenacious to make it in my line of work," I said sheepishly. "Just because I got bit in the ass on this one doesn't mean my job is complete."

He scoffed at me and started for the door. When he got to the door, he turned back to me and regarded me for a moment.

"This will be the thing that makes you," he said before leaving.

I kept hearing Grenadine's parting shot at me the night before and I understood exactly what she meant finally seeing that my actions were already in motion to make her plan work out just as she wanted.

"How bad do you want it?"

Pretty badly, apparently.

CHAPTER SEVENTEEN

I was released from the hospital the very next day. As far as the hospital knew, I was going to Parkersburg to my mother's cramped, smoke filled trailer, but that wasn't happening and my mom knew it. I promised to stay in touch and to take her out to dinner before I went home to Reading, and my mom went away from me quietly and beaten. Grenadine's words to me about my being a bad daughter hit me when my mother left that hospital with her shoulders slumped forward and her head hanging. A momentary stab of guilt hit me, but I was again overcome with the need to make the most of my position. Mom would have to wait.

Anais was able to get a large suite at another nearby hotel and we holed up in there, talking for hours about the version of events to which I was committing myself. Anais was horrified that, according to the web of bullshit I was weaving, I had managed to find and bang the very murderer I had travelled down there to profile. It was true that my luck wasn't reliable or even plentiful, as Anais kept saying, and given that I had been dealing with Grenadine pretty much the entire time I was there and not just having carefree sex with Terry, that was more than enough proof for me that I was carrying an empty bucket when it came to good luck.

"I want to go ahead and write my next entry on the site," I told Anais suddenly. It was still my first day out of the hospital and Anais frowned at me.

"It can wait. I'll update social media and say an emergency has come up and that it will be a few more days until you are able to submit a new entry," she said to me sternly.

"No." I said back. "This is important, Ana. I am not beaten, and I do not want to look beaten. I'll look like a bad judge of character maybe, but think about it! This is going to blow us up. I was almost his next victim! We'll take pictures of my face and body and I'll write about my harrowing ordeal and this will secure our reputation. Nobody will accuse us of fan-girling killers anymore."

"The hell they won't!" Ana shot back. "Girl, you were fucking the killer! People are going to say that it was our foolishness and need to chase this shit that got you raped and beaten up. And Chris, I don't know about you publishing about being raped and beaten. I'm really not comfortable posting pictures of your face either, *mami*."

"We do it to other people all the time," I said calmly. "How can we possibly look like we're unfeeling and opportunistic if we treat my attack like we would any other?"

"We'll look opportunistic because we'll be profiting off of you being raped and beaten!" Anais shouted, throwing her hands in the air in frustration.

"We profit off of the suffering and beatings and rapings and even murders of total strangers, Ana." I was sounding frustrated too, so I sighed and looked Anais in the eyes. "I'll handle it with grace and care. I promise. This isn't going to be a 'look at me!' kind of thing. I wouldn't want that, and this is going to be public knowledge anyhow, you know. I want this file finished and closed."

Anais stared at me, chewing her lower lip like she usually did when she was contemplating a hard call. I cocked an eyebrow at her, wincing when it pulled too hard on a cut on my forehead. I saw Anais wince at my wincing and I winked at her, causing her to scoff at me, smiling indulgently.

"This still makes me uncomfortable," she said, making me smile knowing that I'd won that tug of war.

"Welcome to the other side where it's about more than page hits," I said, feeling stupid because I was very much making my being a victim all about the page hits. It was Grenadine's gift to me and damn it, I was going to use it.

My cell phone started ringing and I was surprised to see that it was a call from Sgt. Blaniar.

"Hello, Ms. Cunningham," he greeted me after I answered. "I'm calling you personally to let you know that Terry Knight has tried to commit suicide. I need you to come down here and have a sit-down with me today, would that be alright?"

Oh shit, I thought.

"Sure," I answered confidently. "When is a good time?"

"The sooner the better, please," he said.

"I'm leaving now," I said.

Anais was looking at me quizzically and when I told her what Sgt. Blaniar had said to me, she offered to drive, which I had to accept anyway because I was still medicated, and driving wasn't safe. The drive from the hotel to the police station took about 15 minutes and Anais was silent the whole time, emanating tension and anxiety. I was glad to get out of a cramped car with her and leave her in a seating area while I was escorted into an intimidating interrogation room. Sgt. Blaniar was waiting for me looking even more tired than the previous day.

"Tell me what happened," I blurted even before sitting down.

"He tried hanging himself with his bedsheets," he answered me blandly. "He was caught, but we aren't equipped to deal with that kind of thing here."

"What kind of thing? Surely, he's not the first guy to get locked up to try that," I said, confused.

"Ms. Cunningham," Sgt. Blaniar said, leaning forward and extending his steepled hands closer to me, "we've had to move Mr. Knight to a mental health facility. He's being sedated and locked down."

"Because of suicide?" I asked, aghast. "Hasn't this state caught up with the times yet? You can't treat competent people that way! You don't lock people away like that just because their will broke!"

Sgt. Blaniar regarded me for a moment, making me very self-conscious about my badly bruised face.

"I want you to watch something," he said, getting up and leaving the room. When he returned, he turned on the television in the room.

On the screen sat Sgt. Blaniar, another man I didn't recognize, and Terry. Terry was handcuffed to a loop sticking out of the tabletop and he was slumped over, head hanging.

"Mr. Knight, can you tell me about the shed in your backyard?" Blaniar asked on the tape.

"It was clean." Terry muttered. "I keep it clean. Always clean. No dirt. No dust. Can't have mice. No, mice are dirty. I never liked Disney because of that mouse. No mice. Who says they're cute? They're not."

"There was blood and bone all over that shed, Mr. Knight," Blaniar said. "Can you tell me about it?"

"Clean. I keep it clean. I paid cash for it and I wouldn't let it get dirty. Her eyes hurt me. Her eyes ate me. I'm eaten. I'm gone. You don't see me. I'm gone."

I saw the two officers glance at each other and shift in their seats.

"Did you know Martin Hamrick or Matthew Hart?" Blaniar asked.

"Eaten," Terry repeated.

"Did you know them?" Blaniar repeated.

"*I AM EATEN. GONE. EATEN,*" Terry screamed, jerking upright and pulling at the chains that attached him to the table.

The two officers jumped in surprise at his outburst but remained seated.

"Did you murder Stephanie D'Agostino?" Blaniar asked. "Did you cut her hands off and put them in the ASPCA building?"

"She overpaid for manicures," Terry said, hanging his head again.

"Is that why you murdered her?" Blaniar asked.

"There are too many sound waves. It's the metal. Metal is bad for people to be surrounded by like this. I am consumed. Again," Terry answered.

Blaniar turned off the television and resumed his seat across from me, looking deeply into me again.

"We questioned him for three hours and he made no more sense the entire time than he did there," he said.

"You think he's faking it?" I asked, my hands wringing on the tabletop.

"He has no history of mental health problems, not even for a prescription for an anti-depressant. We have dozens of people here on the force who knew him as a very average guy. He wasn't sullen or withdrawn and he never displayed anything but typical behavior. Now, I know that I'm grabbing for stereotypes to explain this, but I've never seen someone go from seeming normal to ranting like that and making absolutely no sense quite as fast," Blaniar answered.

"You don't think he's faking," I said. "Is that it?"

"Never mind what I think," he answered, waving a hand at me. "You are someone who saw him more intimately than his coworkers. I want to know if you ever noticed him come unhinged like that before. Did he ever drop off and stop making sense around you?"

"You mean other than when he raped me and beat the hell out of me?" I asked. I wasn't going to shy away from what had happened to me. I was wearing it all over my face anyhow, so I thought that I might as well have been frank about it. My frankness made Sgt. Blaniar wince and shift in his seat.

"No," I said. "He was always this really polite man who never once said a curse word and always offered to pay for meals even when I was the one who suggested going out. He never, ever struck me as a violent person and he sure as hell didn't strike me as a person capable of all of this."

Blaniar was nodding his head while looking down at the table.

"Can I see him?" I asked suddenly. Sgt. Blaniar's head snapped up and he looked at me in shock. "I want to interview him," I continued flatly.

"Absolutely not," he answered just as flatly.

"I have rights," I came back, indignantly. "All I need is the permission of either Terry or his next of kin."

"And I can make sure that you don't get that!" Blaniar shouted at me. "What is the matter with you? Are you really that hungry for attention?"

"It's not for attention," I said, working to retain my composure. "This is my job, Sergeant. This is how I make my living. Now how would it look to the public, a public who has shown in the past to be highly critical and un-approving of what I do, if I let this story go cold when, if the victim were any other person, I would be hunting down all of the interviews that I could? Why, in this case, should the victim be treated more delicately than in the past?"

Blaniar had no reply. He just sat in his hard metal chair staring at me with his eyes open wide and his head shaking from side to side. I assume he was thinking that I was a few pieces short of a complete chess set, but I didn't care.

"What about his shed? I heard someone yelling about it that night," I continued.

Sgt. Blaniar sputtered at me for a moment before he was able to answer me.

"It's the evidence that we need to prove that you're not his only victim," he answered, trying to regain his composure.

"You mention on that video that you found blood and bone in there. How much? It was enough to make someone yell. And when will you be able to test to see if the materials match any of the previous victims?"

He didn't answer me this time. He was sitting back in his chair with his hands lying flat on the table. He was staring at me with a look of complete disgust on his face. I knew I'd overplayed my hand.

"It would make both of our lives easier if you just helped facilitate an interview with Terry for me," I said softly.

"No. Not only is it absolutely not within your goddamn rights, Miss Cunningham, it's vulgar. It is not happening, I don't care how seriously you take your career as a murder groupie with a blog."

Okay, that hurt.

"Sgt. Blaniar, I know that maybe it seems lowly to you, but this is my livelihood."

"Miss Cunningham, my mind will not be changing. The answer will always be no."

He stood then and strode out of the room in a hurry, his disgust with me making him move fast. I should have been used to it. Cops got disgusted with me and told me "no" all the time. I shrugged and made my way to Anais. I had a first-hand account of an attack. I had plenty.

CHAPTER EIGHTEEN

When Anais and I got back into our room, Anais got onto her laptop and started checking emails. I sat and watched her fondly for a few moments before I realized that I was sick to death of being in a hotel.

"I want to go home," I blurted.

"Well it's about fuckin' time." Anais said, slamming her laptop closed. "We'll leave tomorrow morning and be home before dinner."

I nodded. I took a long hot shower, wincing in pain and trying hard to avoid touching the bite marks all over my body. They were in places that were already tender, and it hurt to move in certain ways because of that, but the hot water stinging the wounds felt oddly relaxing. It was like the hot water was eating away at the germs and dirt of what had happened to me. I'd only taken sponge baths after my hospital stay so that I wouldn't disturb that bandaging on the bite marks but taking off those bandages and taking that shower made things immeasurably better.

I took my time standing in front of the big, granite-topped vanity in the bathroom looking at myself. My face was a multi-colored, bruised mess as was my body. The insides of my thighs were purple and there was a bruise on my hip that looked a lot like a thumb, probably where Terry had gripped me. There were tiny cuts all over me from where my clothes had been ripped off and my scalp hurt.

I started crying, looking at the reflection and really letting myself see what had happened to me. Poor Terry, but poor me as well. I was dragged down a hallway by my hair, beaten, and brutally raped. Then I got to endure the shame of having a rape kit done. I'd have nightmares for the rest of my life about Terry's dead eyes as he was on top of me as well as Grenadine and that goddamned scary as hell stew pot of hers.

But, thinking about that stew pot, I knew that I'd gotten off lucky. Look at how all of the other people who'd met up with Grenadine had faired. Skinned, boiled, chopped up, gutted, and added to a giant pot over a roaring fire.

A knock on the door startled a yelp out of me. It was Anais, making sure that I was okay.

"Come on, *mami*," she said, walking me to my bed. "Get some rest. We've got a long drive home tomorrow."

I smiled at her. Anais is Puerto Rican and expertly bilingual, but she only ever says a word or two of Spanish around me since I don't know much more than the few things I learned in Middle School Spanish class. Even when she gets mad and rants she makes sure to mostly speak in English so that I can follow her on her little stream of consciousness. She's awesome like that.

I resolved to try and learn a bit more Spanish when we got home. As a bit of affection to Ana.

I just hoped that that psycho fairy would let me go home.

CHAPTER NINETEEN

It *was* a long drive home, but it was also an uneventful drive that saw both Anais and me arrive safely. A few days later, after a few phone calls to the police (Sgt. Blaniar refused to talk to me anymore), I sat down and recorded my next entry into the file on *Killer Chronicles*. I was surprised at how emotional I became recounting what happened to me and what eventually happened to Terry.

Life blew up for us then. The local paper interviewed us again, with more emphasis on me this time and we got a journalist who wasn't as interested in discrediting us as before. It was great. We looked like serious investigative journalists. I looked like a woman who maybe takes her career too seriously, but ultimately still a victim. That newspaper article was the start of a million big things for Anais and me.

I got offered a book deal from not one, not two, but three publishers who wanted to pay me to write about my experiences. People were eating it up. Young, attractive female journalist goes to small town West Virginia to investigate a series of horrible murders and mutilations and ends up involved with the very murderer and nearly becomes his next victim. Anais took on the role of my manager/agent. She was able to negotiate a five-figure bonus on my book deal as well as a great percentage of per-unit sales. Anais, of course, got a great cut of this and when movie studios came sniffing around after the book made it onto all of the best seller lists, she was able to negotiate another monumentally sweet deal. On top of all of that, *Killer Chronicles*, our beloved little site, was bought out by a major media corporation and is still functioning smoothly to this day. Anais stayed on as a moderator and editor and I do guest posts on it every once in a while so that people don't forget where I got my start.

Needless to say, Anais and I were finally able to afford getting our own places. Ana moved to a part of town that is seeing mostly new construction. Her family came to Reading from New York and they knew only meager homes, so moving into a place where everything is all new really appealed to her. I cried when she moved, and I missed having her just a room away at all times, but we've stayed close. I bought and restored an old brick house that is walking distance from some great restaurants so that I can eat well and still make sure I get all of my footsteps in.

I also made sure to take care of my mom. I moved her out of that trailer park and into a small but well-insulated home with central air. To her, it's fancy as hell. She also gets a monthly check and I try not to let it bother me that she's using it to buy Misty's and beer. My mom should spend the twilight of her life in comfort, I guess. It's no real hardship on me to just cut a check anyhow. What really matters to me is that that crap Grenadine said to me is no longer true.

Terry. Poor Terry was proven to be incompetent to stand trial for his crimes and will live the rest of his life in a mental hospital. It's a shame, but bad luck swung his way. There's really not much I can do for him except try to make sure to mention what a gentle and kind man he was before he attacked me. It doesn't mean much, especially since that version of events has made me a fairly wealthy woman. At least he doesn't know better. This way he can't hate me. Or discredit me.

I haven't been visited by that fairy again. I guess once she paid me my "favor" she was done with me. I'm not complaining. It wasn't exactly fun listening to her talk about being a superior being before her deteriorated mind short-circuited and she'd smack the hell out of me. I'm just happy to be out of her sights.

I'm a success. Terry is locked up and I'm in therapy, but my reputation is set, and I will live my life as a person with a respected name in my field. That is important to me. I want to be respected and successful. It had a price, but what doesn't in this life? It wasn't like I set out to look for a favor from a crazy fairy. It landed in my lap and even though some of the consequences were steep, I'm still going to milk this opportunity for all it's worth. It would be a shame not to.

So, who's the monster in this situation? My first answer, and the one that I would think is most obvious, is Grenadine. But I stop sometimes, and I think about how things played out and how this story actually played out for me and I have to wonder if that's true. What kind of person is thankful to have met a supernatural being because, even though several lives were ruined, it meant success and validation? A monster? A sociopathic narcissist? Whatever the label, I'm terribly afraid sometimes that it's me. I'm that thing. My therapist tries to assure me that I'm just numbing myself to the horrible guilt I feel, but what the hell does she know? I can't tell her the whole story. It's not guilt that numbs me. It's the fear of an absence of guilt.

When I think back to the last time Grenadine spoke to me, her face inches from mine and her black eyes practically laughing at me and my pain, I understand that she knew me better than I'd ever want to admit out loud. All of that torturous time that she took in thinking about what would be an appropriate favor to pay me in response to the Nummy Nellie snack cake that she stole from me was well-spent. That supernatural being set out to pay me a hell of a favor and she did. She asked the question, but she knew the answer.

I wanted it *real* bad.

And I still eat and enjoy the hell out of my Nummy Nellie cakes. No one can take that from me.

-END-

ABOUT THE AUTHOR

Somer Canon is a minivan-revving suburban mother who avoids her neighbors for fear of being found out as a weirdo. When she's not peering out of her windows, she's consuming books, movies, and video games that sate her need for blood, gore, and things that disturb her mother.

ALSO FROM
BLOODSHOT BOOKS

From a crater lake on an island off the coast of Bronze Age Estonia...

To a crippled Viking warrior's conquest of England ...

To the bloody temple of an Aztec god of death and resurrection...

Their presence has shaped our world. They are the Riders.

One month ago, an urban explorer was drawn to an abandoned asylum in the mountains of northern Massachusetts. There he discovered a large specimen jar, containing something organic, unnatural and possibly alive.

Now, he and a group of unsuspecting individuals have discovered one of history's most horrific secrets. Whether they want to or not, they are caught in the middle of a millennia-old war and the latest battle is about to begin.

Available in paperback or Kindle on Amazon.com
http://amzn.to/1peMAjz

FINALLY IN PRINT AFTER MORE THAN THREE DECADES, THE NOVEL MARK MORRIS WROTE <u>BEFORE</u> *TOADY*

EVIL NEEDS ONLY A SEED

Limefield has had more than its fair share of tragedy. Barely six years ago, a disturbed young boy named Russell Swaney died beneath the wheels of a passenger train mere moments after committing a heinous act of unthinkable sadism. Now, a forest fire caused by the thoughtless actions of two teens has laid waste to hundreds of acres of the surrounding woodlands and unleashed a demonic entity

EVIL TAKES ROOT

Now, a series of murders plague the area and numerous local residents have been reported missing, including the entire population of the nearby prison. But none of this compares to the appearance of the Winter Tree, a twisted wooden spire which seems to leech the warmth from the surrounding land.

EVIL FLOURISHES

Horrified by what they have caused, the two young men team up with a former teacher and the local police constabulary to find the killer, but it may already be too late. Once planted, evil is voracious. Like a weed, it strangles all life, and the roots of the Winter Tree are already around their necks.

Available in paperback or Kindle on Amazon.com

http://bit.ly/TreeKindle

There's a monster coming to the small town of Pikeburn. In half an hour, it will begin feeding on the citizens, but no one will call the authorities for help. They are the ones who sent it to Pikeburn. They are the ones who are broadcasting the massacre live to the world. Every year, Red Diamond unleashes a new creation in a different town as a display of savage terror that is part warning and part celebration. Only no one is celebrating in Pikeburn now. No one feels honored or patriotic. They feel like prey.

Local Sheriff Yan Corban refuses to succumb to the fear, paranoia, and violence that suddenly grips his town. Stepping forward to battle this year's lab-grown monster, Sheriff Corban must organize a defense against the impossible. His allies include an old art teacher, a shell-shocked mechanic, a hateful millionaire, a fearless sharpshooter, a local meth kingpin, and a monster groupie. Old grudges, distrust, and terror will be the monster's allies in a game of wits and savagery, ambushes and treachery. As the conflict escalates and the bodies pile up, it becomes clear this creature is unlike anything Red Diamond has unleashed before.

No mercy will be asked for or given in this battle of man vs monster. It's time to run, hide, or fight. It's time for Red Diamond.

Available in paperback or Kindle on Amazon.com

http://bit.ly/DiamondUS

January 12, 1888

When a day dawns warm and mild in the middle of a long cold winter, it's greeted as a blessing, a reprieve. A chance for those who've been cooped up indoors to get out, do chores, run errands, send the children to school... little knowing that they're only seeing the calm before the storm.

The blizzard hits out of nowhere, screaming across the Great Plains like a runaway train. It brings slicing winds, blinding snow, plummeting temperatures. Livestock will be found frozen in the fields, their heads encased in blocks of ice formed from their own steaming breath. Frostbite and hypothermia wait for anyone caught without shelter.

For the hardy settlers of Far Enough, in the Montana Territory, it's about to get worse. Something else has arrived with the blizzard. Something sleek and savage and hungry. Wild animal or vengeful spirit from native legend, it blends into the snow and bites with sharper teeth than the wind.

It is called the *wanageeska*.

It is the White Death

http://bit.ly/WDKindle

ON THE HORIZON FROM
BLOODSHOT BOOKS

2018*

Victoria (What Hides Within #2) – Jason Parent

2019-20*

Bleed Away the Sky – Brian Fatah Steele
The Devil Virus – Chris DiLeo
What Sleeps Beneath – John Quick
The Cryptids – Elana Gomel
Dead Sea Chronicles – Tim Curran
Midnight Solitaire – Greg F. Gifune
Dead Branches – Benjamin Langley
The October Boys – Adam Millard
Clownflesh – Tim Curran
Blood Mother: A Novel of Terror – Pete Kahle
Not Your Average Monster – World Tour
The Abomination (The Riders Saga #2) – Pete Kahle
The Horsemen (The Riders Saga #3) – Pete Kahle

other titles to be added when confirmed

BLOODSHOT BOOKS

READ UNTIL YOU BLEED!

CPSIA information can be obtained
at www.ICGtesting.com
Printed in the USA
LVHW041630060319
609715LV00003B/510